# ROUGH TRIP

SCREAMING DEMONS MC
BOOK SEVEN

## SUMMER COOPER
## SIENNA CHANCE

LOVY BOOKS

It had been days since Sage and his team were deployed out into the field in Afghanistan. He felt like they had walked miles upon miles every day in a never-ending dry land. The sun had not helped as it constantly hung above them day in and day out like a predator waiting for its prey to die after it had struck. The heat had started drying out the water that had remained in their systems since their last sip, which had started to feel like months ago instead of just a few hours. Sage kept picturing himself back at home in the pool in his backyard, surrounded by clean and fresh water. The thought of it didn't help him, though because he started to feel like his skin was tightening from the dehydration. He started to feel as though he was literally a fish out of water.

"This heat is killing me," Jason said. Jason had been a

private for a while now, and Sage would never understand why. He complained about everything which he found irritating, as did the rest of the team.

"It's killing us all," Ryan said. He had always been the forward one in the group, never batting an eyelid when it came to being honest. Everyone laughed at his statement, everyone except Jason, of course.

"You don't have to be such a dick, Ryan," Jason said as he glared at Ryan, who had his back to him.

"I'm not being a dick, I'm just saying what everyone else is thinking."

"Now, now, children. There's no need to fight," Laura said. Everyone could hear she had a smile on her face as her voice had sounded playful.

"Exactly, Jason, no need to fight, child," Ryan said.

"Oi, cut it out. The lot of you!" the sergeant yelled. "You're all acting like children. Lord knows why you even bothered joining the army with the attitudes you lot have," he said.

"Sorry, Sir," Jason said with a sarcastic salute since the sergeant was in the lead facing away from everyone. Jason had always had a problem with the sergeant, no one ever knew why.

"Yeah, sorry, Sir," Ryan said.

"Yeah, yeah. Now shut your mouths. We aren't out here for fun!"

Sage could agree with him there. He would rather be

back home. Again he pictured himself in his pool or better yet watching a game on TV while having a cold beer. That would also be great, Sage thought.

At the thought of a cold beer, Sage recognized just how dry his mouth had become. He was sure that all of their mouths had become so dry it felt like sandpaper rubbing against their gums every time they tried to bring saliva back; none of them were used to such dry climates. The heat wasn't as much of a problem as the dryness was; the dryness was almost unbearable.

They had been surrounded by sand, dust and run-down buildings most of the time. Everything dried out and ready to just dissolve into nothingness. Sage was certain that soon, his body and everyone else on the team's bodies would dissolve into nothingness from the dehydration.

The wind was constantly bringing a whip of dust across their faces, making their faces look dirty and dry during their walks. It felt like their skin would just start cracking at any moment.

They hadn't seen people for miles, and they had started to doubt that they would. There wasn't much reported civilization left that far out; they had either been killed or told to leave. Sage had wished that they hadn't come this far out. He knew the job they had to do but it was so far away from anything that it started to look like those abandoned towns that he'd seen in movies just before zombies and monsters started attacking. He had always had an imaginative mind, and although he wasn't exactly scared, he couldn't help but wonder why anyone would come this far when it just felt dangerous.

They had to continue to look for a group of insurgents that had been reportedly shooting at teams while they were out patrolling the area, they had even shot at civilians. It had been their mission to shoot at any threats that may appear. They could not risk losing any more men than they already had.

"Take cover ladies. We can't risk being seen," the sergeant said to the team.

Why does he always call us ladies, Sage thought, it had always frustrated him. Maybe it was to show superiority or something, but it had just made the team dislike him. The sergeant had been belittling the crew from the beginning, although they had fought alongside him a few times, and he had hand-picked them to be his team. They had all been trained to meet his standards, and he had trained them hard, drilling the team every day at unexpected times. It had done them all good. Expect the unexpected.

Sage had constantly kept a close eye on Laura, it had been the hardest thing to accept when they had been called out for the mission.

He could remember the day he had asked her to stay

behind, but she had told him she would not stay behind when her team would be out in the field. It had been her duty to fight with her team.

*"Sage, please do not ask me to stay behind. This is what I signed up for when I joined the army. How would it look if you went and I stayed here? We're both privates, and I have to stay with my team,"* she had said.

*"How can you expect me to be okay with you there? You don't have to go. Please, just think about it."*

*"I know I don't have to go, but I need to fight with my brothers, I need to fight for my country."*

*"Laura, anything could happen while we're out there."*

*"And anything could happen while you're out there and I'm here, waiting for you to come home. I couldn't sit and wait for either good or bad news, Sage. I joined before I met you and I'm very lucky to have met you, but this is not something I can just walk away from. This is my duty."*

Sage knew fighting alongside her would not be easy. He felt he had to make sure she was constantly safe although he knew she could look after herself. She was on his team, after all, and had been trained with him but fighting in a war with the love of your life would not be easy for anyone placed in the same shoes as Sage. He didn't want to imagine a life without her in it. He hoped that this mission would go smoothly so they could be in and out.

"Keep close; we're coming to an open area. Keep alert

and aware of your surroundings," the sergeant commanded.

As they started to move forward they all ducked under anything they could to keep low and covered. They started weaving in and out of empty buildings, looking for any signs of life and possible movement. There didn't appear to be any. Most of the buildings that surrounded them had already been blown up or shot through, the walls were half gone with wide holes here and there, and they had to almost crawl on their bellies across the ground to stay covered. Besides their breathing and footsteps, there were no other sounds, the saying 'silence can be deafening' came to Sage's mind.

It had started to feel too quiet, there should be at least a few people out here Sage thought.

They continued to move forward, after all, there was no going back. Moving slowly and carefully, making sure that their foot movement could hardly be heard. They came to a higher wall where they could stand straighter. Just as they all started to stand up straighter, gunshots started to ring out across the empty buildings, echoing across the empty area that surrounded them.

They started out distant and soft but as the firing picked up, soon the crackling sounds of bullets hitting cement would be the only thing anyone could hear. The team started looking around, searching for the main source of fire.

"Laura, stay low!" Sage yelled as the ringing in his ears got louder. He couldn't risk her getting shot.

The team had begun to fire shots in all directions, hoping that they were shooting at the source as they were still rather clueless as to where the shots were coming from.

"Fall back!" the sergeant yelled, "stay low. Get as low to the ground and as close to a wall as possible!"

Shit, Sage thought, this can't be happening. The team ducked down, again almost on their bellies as they tried to take cover.

It had been made out to be an easy mission. Go in, get to the group of insurgents, take care of them and then get out. Simple. Nothing was ever simple though.

The ringing in Sage's ears had become deafening; he was certain he had lost his hearing as the firing started to sound muffled. He could see the mouths of his teammates moving around him but he could no longer hear what they were saying. The remains of the walls around them started crumbling to the ground, soon there would be no walls at all and they would be completely exposed. The dust and sand had started to kick back into their eyes as bullets continued to fly in their direction.

Sage looked around them; there was nowhere else to hide. They were going to die, and when he looked at his teammates' faces he knew they knew it too. They kept firing and reloading their weapons in the hopes that they could at least injure the enemy.

He looked over at Laura and could see the look of panic written all over her face. He looked around him and forced himself to focus. He could see at least one shooter in the distance so he wasted no time and shot directly at them, taking them down with just a few hits.

One down, a couple dozen to go, he thought. The team followed his lead and tried to focus on targets to shoot at instead of just all over the place in their panic. Slowly they began to fight back properly, but the insurgents had them surrounded. They had planned this attack so thoroughly that the chances of survivors were slim. The sergeant had already radioed in for reinforcements but that would take a while and they all knew it. They were stuck on their own and the only way out would be to fight back - this is what they had been trained for.

Sage continued to fire at any target he could see, he had to try. Constantly turning this way and that to get a better angle of their attackers.

"Jason! On your right!" he yelled. Jason took note and turned to his left, shooting the target. Soon they all worked together and yelled out targets for each other, forming a circle with their guns pointing out and their backs pressed against each other.

He looked in one direction and saw a grenade heading toward them.

"Everybody move!" he yelled. They all looked in the direction he was looking, seeing the grenade they all tried to move out of the way, running as far out of the area and yet there was nowhere for them to go.

Sage headed for Laura. If he were to die, he would die next to her.

He had gotten to her just as the grenade landed in the center of the group, causing them all to be pushed further back in every direction.

Sage was engulfed in darkness.

He could feel the wind blowing around him, he could feel it tugging at his hair as he came to. The more he became aware of his surroundings, he could hear people yelling and a high pitched whistling noise ringing in his ears.

As he regained full consciousness he could feel an enormous amount of pain flood through his body and became so overwhelmed that he couldn't help but yell out in agony.

Someone close heard him scream and rushed over.

"You're okay private!" a young male said as he leaned over him so his head popped into view. "You're on your way to Charité, a hospital in Germany. They're going to take care of you," the person yelled. As Sage's sense became clearer he realized his head was restrained and his body had been tied down so he couldn't move. He also realized he was on a helicopter. That could only mean that help had come after the grenade knocked him out.

"Laura? Where is Laura?" he started to ask. He tried to break free from the restraints that held his body down.

"Private, please. You need to stay calm and you need to stay still!" the person yelled over the sound of the rotors.

"Where is Laura?" he cried. He looked around him and couldn't see anyone else from his team. How many people could fit on a helicopter while on a gurney, he asked himself.

It wasn't long till the helicopter landed and he was rushed into the E.R.

"Laura? Laura?" Sage continued to ask once he had gained his consciousness again.

"Private Anderson, my name is Dr. Müller. I worked on your head in surgery. You suffered a blow to your head, shards from the grenade that had blown up near you hit you on the right side of your head. You'll have a scar there for the rest of your life, about 4 inches long but you will survive," the doctor said.

He registered a pounding in his head, he reached his hand up and touched his face. He felt the bandage wrapped around the side of his face and proceeded to wince a bit as he applied pressure to the bandaged area. Stupid idea, he thought.

Sage then looked around him, taking in his surroundings. White walls and clean beds all with their curtains tied back. The smell of medicine in the air. Machines beeping and people coughing in the far distance.

He zoned in on one detail - the beds. All clean beds he noticed, clean, empty beds.

"My team? Where is my team? Where is Laura?" he asked, panic rising in his voice.

"Private Anderson, I'm sorry to inform you but you're the only one who made it," the doctor said.

"No, no don't tell me that," Sage said as tears started filling his eyes.

"I'm so sorry, Private."

Sage closed his eyes as tears started streaming down his face. She was gone, Laura was gone and he would never get her back. He would never say goodbye, he would never kiss her, touch her or hear her voice ever again. His chest began to feel tight and he felt a pain deep within.

Why had he survived? He should be with his team. He should be with his team and not in the hospital getting patched up. How could he be the only survivor? He didn't deserve to be alive.

"Please leave me alone. I need to be alone," he said.

He could not bear being so vulnerable around people. He felt as if his whole world had crumbled around him.

"Yes, of course. Please press the red button next to your bed if you need any assistance," the doctor said as he turned to leave and closed the door behind him.

Sage was left in the room by himself as he broke down and sobbed for the loss of his team, the loss of Laura.

1

---

**3 years ago**

$\mathcal{I}$t had been two years since the attack in Afghanistan. Sage had managed to get his life back in order and his head healed although he was left with a scar. His heart had never been able to fully recover from the loss. He still had the constant feeling that he needed to protect something, to fight for something. It had been the one thing he had been trained to do and that sort of training never goes away, even after everything he had been through. He had been in and out of security jobs until he had found Hamilton. Having the opportunity to join the Screaming Demons was not something he could easily just walk away from. It was a once in a lifetime opportunity and he took it with both hands.

It was the first time Sage entered the Screaming Demons bar. He had no idea how well the meeting with Max would go. He wouldn't walk into a place like that without doing his research first. He liked to be prepared. He liked to know who he was dealing with. And this place, the people who ran this place, were not people he wanted to be on the wrong side of.

The place had a rundown, old school look about it. The walls were half mahogany with bricks going toward the ceiling, generously lined with photographs that looked like they had been taken at least 30 odd years before, completely vintage looking. The light fixtures hung low from the ceiling, with dim bulbs to create a dark and mysterious atmosphere which suited the Screaming Demons perfectly. There was a large mahogany bar just off-center from the entrance that had ceiling to floor shelves filled with only the finest liquors around the world. The Screaming Demons had to have the best there was and Sage knew that. And although there were a few stools at the bar, the place had mostly booths that were covered in pure leather and detailed to perfection; each booth looked plush and extremely comfortable. The bar itself would never be filled to the brim but there would always be just enough people to make it buzz like a hornet's nest.

Sage decided to take a seat at the bar as he waited for Hamilton who had gone to speak to Grier, and Sage had been ordered to wait for their return. He had thought about ordering a drink. A whiskey neat would be great but Sage knew better than to drink on the job. Also, he had laid off the booze for quite some time so it wouldn't be smart to start as he was just entering a new job.

"Anything I can get for you?" the bartender asked as she approached Sage from across the bar.

"Oh, nothing for me thanks. I'm here for Hamilton," Sage said.

The bartender who had fiery red hair nodded knowingly. "All right," she said as she walked back to the other side of the bar.

"Sage, over here! Max is expecting you," Hamilton shouted and the room went quiet. All the Demons watched as Sage slowly dragged his body across the room, passing all the Demons, toward Max's office. He could feel each one of them, breathing down his neck, sniffing him, checking him out. He knew they couldn't touch him. Not when he was there to meet their king. Not until he'd had a chance to prove his worth to their club.

"We could use a man with your skill," Max coughed while pointing at the whiskey at the table. The woman next to him quickly poured him a glass and at the same time threw him a you-shouldn't-be-drinking-this look.

"Just do what you're told," Max took the glass and signaled Sage to leave the room. Those words were for him as much as the woman. Max was an undeniable genius, he chuckled to himself.

Unlike the other Demons, his first meeting with Max was short and kind of sweet in that there was no blood-shed. Max was too exhausted to even look at him for another second. Maybe he didn't care about the club anymore as he was dying. Maybe he trusted Hamilton, his judgment of character.

Either way, that was ancient history…

Now… he works for Fiona.

* * *

"WHAT CAN I GET YOU?" a female voice asked from behind him.

As Sage turned around, he saw a pair of brown eyes looking straight at him. The brown eyes glistened with mischief, and he sensed trouble. As he continued to examine the rest of the face he noted a head of short black hair, with slight flicks at the ends just meeting the female's collarbone, freckles splattered across the bridge of her nose going slightly onto her cheeks and small, pixie-like ears popping out of the sides. Although her eyes were just brown Sage couldn't help but be slightly captivated by them. They looked like pools of honey; he could probably get lost in them for hours and he knew that that could be bad news. It took him a while to bring himself back into the moment. He had almost lost track of where he was.

"Where's Autumn?"

"She's gone to a different chapter. I'm her replacement."

"Since when?" Sage moved closer to the woman as if interrogating her. She moved even closer in response and he could now smell her perfume.

"Mmm… a few weeks ago," Sage had been busying himself, pretending to sleep through the Wall Kats and the Hell Kats, he didn't notice they had a new girl working at the bar.

"So what will it be, big guy?" she said with a cheeky wink, bringing him back to reality.

"And who are you exactly?" Sage asked. Danger, he thought to himself. He could already sense that she would be bad news for him if he were to get involved and the one thing he knew about himself was that he was never wrong. There had only been a few times where he didn't listen to his instinct and he had learned his lesson.

"The name is Mia, but you can call me whatever you like, sexy," she said with a cheeky grin that showed off a perfect set of white teeth.

He couldn't help but smile at her little grin.

She oozed confidence and sex appeal.

"You done with your questions?" Sage could tell she was part of the Hell Kats and he knew how they worked, a little too well. Messing around with the Kats was one thing, having a close relationship with one was another. He knew he couldn't get too close.

"Don't you have better things to do?" Sage asked. She hadn't moved, she had taken a seat next to him at the bar and rested her head in her hands and stared at him while she leaned on the bar with her elbows.

"Well, I could be doing you but I think that's still up for discussion," Mia said with yet another wink.

Sage chuckled. "Someone is coming in hot."

He would be lying to himself if he said he didn't like her attitude. Although she came across as cute, or rather she looked cute, he could tell she had a bit of a feisty side. He liked it but he had to keep his head straight. He wasn't here to get involved with anyone, he already knew how that could go. He had a job to do and that had to be all he focused on.

"I'm only matching the heat that's radiating off of you," she said. She seemed to have a sharp tongue and a quick mind.

"Do you have a handbook of sayings hidden some-where?" he asked.

"I can't help myself, you bring it out of me," she replied.

"Haha, see you around," Sage said as he saw Fiona call him over.

Sage had had to pop into the bar more frequently the more he worked for Fiona. Sometimes she'd send him there without her to get files from Grier.

He would be shadowed by Mia every time he went. She seemed to have taken a liking to him and she made it very obvious. And he hadn't taken any interest in any other Kats since he saw her.

*"So it's another day, what can I help you with?" she asked the next time he was at the bar.*

*"You never quit, do you?' he asked. He could have felt irritated by her constantly at his side but instead, he rather liked her following him around.*

*"Not when I want something," she said. "And you're something I want."*

*"I'm not something you should want," he said.*

*"I'll be the judge of that," she replied.*

*Clearly, she would not give up any time soon.*

*Although Sage liked the attention she gave him, he knew couldn't allow himself to feel anything for her. He would not allow himself to. The last time he had fallen in love he had lost it all and it had taken him a long time to recover from that. He could not put himself through that again, especially in this line of work; it was even more messed up than the army ever was. He still missed Laura every day and he could never see himself getting mixed up with anyone again.*

Mia was fierce and beautiful; he definitely had thought about them together but he had to keep his distance. He could not risk getting his heart torn apart. After Laura had died, he could not put himself in a position to lose someone important to him again. It had taken everything he had just to survive after the attack, it had taken everything just to feel normal again.

## 2

Since Mia had joined the Hell Kats she knew she was there only to get intel for the Omens but she had never had to sell her body for anything before and she couldn't bring herself to do that now. She had done a lot of things in her life but she could never feel comfortable sleeping with someone she didn't truly care about or love. She had been caught up with the wrong people all her life and now she had put herself in a life-threatening situation. She only had herself to blame; she had found the Omens and had agreed to be their spy. No one had forced her into it, she had just run out of options and had to do it. Another problem she began to face was that she felt like she belonged with the Hell Kats and she didn't want to lose that. Although they demanded to be known and respected around town, they treated everyone within their group like family, and for Mia, that was all she had ever wanted. She didn't want to risk it by being a spy anymore.

She had managed to flirt her way up and luckily for her, it didn't seem to be that much of an issue. She wasn't sure if it was because of her personality or what but Fiona hadn't said anything to her and she hoped it would stay that way because she couldn't afford to lose her position. She couldn't let the Omens down because she knew her life was on the line. They didn't care if you were a woman; if they didn't get what they wanted, they would make you pay and Mia could only imagine what that would mean for her as she was their strongest lead. She was the only person that had gotten this far and yet she still had nothing to show for it.

She had wanted to get out for so long now, but she could never find out how she could do it without putting herself in danger. They would never just let her walk away, she knew too much.

They would kill her. She knew that was a fact. She couldn't die. She had no idea what to do.

Mia had never meant to develop feelings for Sage, but she could never take her eyes off of him whenever he was around. She had tried to keep her distance but whenever he was around she felt drawn to him like a moth to a flame. It didn't help that he had been coming around more often now that he was one of Fiona's top guys.

His blue eyes were so mesmerizing, and the way he presented himself just screamed strong and protective. She just wanted to have him all to herself but he kept denying her and she couldn't understand why. She knew about him and the other Kats, oh yes, women talk. She also knew he was a gentleman despite the slutty-man-whore act he tried to put on in front of the boys.

She had caught him staring at her which he denied if she ever pointed it out but she couldn't help but think he liked her too.

Mia had flirted with Sage so much and although he smiled and replied to her comments, he would never flirt back. He would flirt with other Kats but never with her. But she was not going to give up easily.

"Hello, big guy," she said as she saw him walk into the bar.

"Hello, you little minx," he replied. Mia couldn't help but laugh.

"Little minx?" she asked.

"Well, yes, I'm sure you know it's true," he replied.

Thinking about it she knew he wasn't wrong.

"This minx wants something that you have," she said.

"And what would that be?" Sage asked.

"You, of course."

"Good luck with that," he said with a chuckle.

"Trust me, Sage, I always get what I want," she said as she turned her back and left.

## 3

Mia hadn't been able to sleep with anyone which meant she had no information for the Omens. She had never realized how hard it would be once she had decided to work with them. She thought that when she took the job and got into the Hell Kats, everything would just fall into place. She never knew she would have to sleep with someone to get information and that task was not something she wanted to complete. It wasn't just the lying that was hard but having to pretend to be someone she wasn't had started to chip away at her. She could barely look at herself in the mirror. She had tried her best to look into other options for finding out anything that she could use but she had come up empty-handed. She knew there was no other way and she had run out of time. She had no more excuses.

"You've been told to get new information for us and you're here empty-handed. How are we supposed to bring down the Screaming Demons when you prove to be so useless?" the informant said.

"I'm sorry but there isn't any new information," she lied, it was the only thing she could do. They couldn't find out why she hadn't found out any information. They'd laugh in her face if they knew.

"You're lying, there has to be something you know," he shouted at her.

"I don't know anything. I swear. They've been cautious around me because I'm new," she lied again.

"Well, you've put yourself in quite a situation now, haven't you?" he said.

Mia did not know the guy who had been sent to meet her but looking into his eyes she could tell that this was going to end badly. He looked at her like she was meat and he hadn't eaten for days. She knew better than to run, she would never be fast enough.

"I don't even understand why they sent you in, you're not even that pretty," he said.

"It's not about looks, it's about building trust," she stated.

"Clearly you haven't done a good job then if you have nothing for us."

"Building trust takes time, but I think I'm getting closer and closer," she lied for the third time. She was trying to bide her time, although she knew it wouldn't matter. She was screwed either way she looked at it.

"You know what the boss is like. He won't be happy that you have nothing for us," he replied.

Mia had met Tyler once, when she had first found the Omens. He was a scary guy, and she was definitely scared for her life.

"I'm sorry, I'm really trying," she said. Tears started building up at her eyes as she came to the realization that she may not walk out of this alive. She knew she was out of excuses and sorry wouldn't work anymore. She had reached the final deadline.

"You're not trying hard enough!" he yelled at her.

"They are very cautious as to who they share information with," she tried again to explain her lack of information.

"You're there to crack them, you're there to get the information no matter what it takes!" he shouted as anger filled his eyes.

If only he knew what it took, she thought. He'd probably enjoy it if she had to sleep with him. She could tell when he first arrived that he was looking her up and down, sizing her up. She didn't understand why at the time but the reason was about to become very obvious the closer he got to her. It's not that he had found her attractive, she thought because he clearly didn't. He was checking to see if she could fight him back. She knew she could not and he definitely knew that too.

Mia knew what it took to get the information they demanded, she just couldn't do it.

She had always tried, she had tried to pick someone and just go with it but every time she would progress she pulled away. She could never sleep with someone for information and she knew it. She wasn't a slut, she had never had to put herself in a position to act like one before and so she just couldn't force herself to do it. She knew the risk though, it was staring at her now right there in front of her.

He started zoning in on her, pushing her up against one of the walls by her throat, tightening his one hand around her throat while his other hand rested against the wall. He pulled her off the wall only to push her back against it, making sure her head got a bit of a hit. He laughed as she winced from the pain coming from the back of her head.

"You've let Tyler down for the last time!" he yelled in her face, some of his spit landing on her cheek as she had turned her face to the side, not wanting to look at him that close. He couldn't have been that much older than Mia, probably 26 or 27. He had a head of brown hair and brown eyes that looked black in the light. Mia took note of his face, which was half-covered with a beard. His face was rather round, although he was muscular, and he reeked of stale beer. Clearly, he had had a few beers before their meeting, though it didn't alter his strength.

"You were warned when you agreed to be a spy, you knew your job and you still did nothing! You're a useless little girl and Tyler doesn't want you around anymore," he said with an evil glimmer in his eyes. She could sense her pending death lingering in the air, she could almost taste it at the back of her mouth as her breathing had started to change due to the tightness around her neck.

The meeting had taken place in an alleyway in a rundown area of town. Extremely dodgy and well known for gang murders, this was an area she knew no one would care if they heard screaming for they had heard it all before. She had nowhere to go and she knew she could not defend herself. Her legs already felt like jelly as she hung just off the ground slowly losing her breath; she didn't have a chance. Her head had already begun to spin after the first little blow to the wall and furthermore, with the lack of oxygen, she knew she wasn't strong enough to take a beating. She had never had to learn how to fight before. He looked at her with a grin of victory and she knew she was dead meat. She closed her eyes and waited for the first blow.

He let her go as he brought his left arm forward for the first swing. He focused on the right side of her face, knocking her to the ground so he could then kick her in her rib cage. Pain shot through the side of her face, connecting with the pain she had already begun to feel in the back from the wall. Her head was pounding and she couldn't focus on anything other than the pain that started radiating from her side. She had closed her eyes so tightly that when she tried to open them again to get a look around her, all she could see was literal stars and darkness. Had she gone blind, she asked herself.

"Please!" she yelled as the pain started becoming too overwhelming for her to handle.

"You have to deal with the consequences," he said as he kicked her again, knocking the wind out of her completely this time.

She was almost so completely distracted by the pain and the blindness in her eyes that she had almost forgotten where she was until the second kick rocked her body. She then tried to curl up into a ball to make it harder for him to kick her again but that just pissed him off even more as he then brought another fist down on her face, still focusing on the right side as that was the side exposed after she had fallen to the ground. She brought her hand up to her face, trying to protect herself from another hit, she opened her eyes and just as she regained her eyesight she could see him getting his foot ready to kick her again.

She had come close to dying only once in her life and she had been grateful she had forgotten most of it. This, however, if she survived, she'd remember for the rest of her life. The pain had become unbearable. She wished she had just been knocked out so hard from the first blow that she wouldn't have to experience getting beaten by a man who didn't even know her; she didn't even know his name.

Just as he began to swing his foot around to kick her for a third time, someone stepped out of the darkness and tackled him to the ground. It was Sage. How had he found her, she asked herself. She struggled to look up as she watched Sage beat the guy. He would kill him if he didn't stop soon, she thought. Although she really shouldn't have cared if he died or not, she couldn't let Sage kill someone for her. That was a bit too much.

Sage proceeded to punch the guy numerous times, making him regret ever laying a hand on Mia.

"Sage, I think that's enough," Mia said as she slowly started to peel herself off of the ground, wincing every time she moved. He hadn't slowed down with his punches even after the guy lay motionless. Sage took notice of what she had said and then jumped off the guy. Breathing heavily as he looked at his blood-covered hands.

He looked around at her and pulled a pained look. Did her face look that bad, she thought. He bent down and helped her up, allowing her to lean on him for support. She could barely walk. Sage attempted to pick her up and help her but she complained that it hurt more so she just hobbled next to him out of the alleyway, leaving the unknown Omen guy there to die.

"Come on," he said, "let's go get you cleaned up." She could only imagine what she looked like.

Sage took her back to his place where he cleaned up her cut lip and the gash on her face. She looked at herself in the mirror; she looked like a hot mess. She had blood pooled in her hair which she'd need a shower to wash out and half of her face was swollen and had already started to bruise. She looked at her neck which also had bruising in the form of fingers starting to develop around her entire neck. She knew she would have no luck hiding any of her injuries and she'd probably have to lay low for a bit until they faded.

"How are your ribs feeling?" he asked as he gently put pressure on her side.

She winced. "I don't know if anything is broken because it hurts like hell."

"Does it hurt when you breathe?" he asked.

"No, not really," she said as she attempted to take a deep breath in. It hurt a little but not too bad.

"That's a good sign then, you should be fine."

"Sage, how did you know I was there?" Mia asked.

"I know everything."

"Were you following me?"

"No… not exactly," Sage looked down, avoiding eye contact with Mia.

"Then?"

"Well it's a good thing I was there or who knows where you'd be right now," he said completely brushing off the question at hand.

"Tell me!" Mia's eyes were staring at Sage so hard that her eyeballs looked like they would pop out of her sockets.

"Alright! I tracked your phone."

"What do you mean? Like 007 shit?"

"Yes, like 007 shit if that's what you want to call it."

Mia rolled her eyes. "Why?"

Sage wasn't going to answer that. He didn't know himself why he did it in the first place.

"I'm asking you a question!"

"I was worried about you."

Mia smiled, obviously pleased with what she'd heard.

Mia shuddered at the thought of what could have happened. She definitely would not be sitting in Sage's house, that's for sure. She was so out of it that she had completely forgotten that she was in Sage's house. She would have preferred it if it had been under better circumstances but she couldn't change that now. She started to look around his apartment.

Typical bachelor pad, she thought. He had kept it rather minimal. There was a couch, a TV and a coffee table in his lounge, a small dining table in the dining room and Mia noticed he didn't have a dishwasher in his kitchen, also no dirty dishes in the sink. Did he always wash his dishes straight after using them, she wondered.

"Thank you, for rescuing me," she said deciding that the question was better left unanswered. "I don't think I would be alive right now if it weren't for you. You saved my life and I owe you so much for that," she said as tears started streaming down her cheeks.

"Hey, come on now. There's no reason to cry," he said as he gently wiped her tears away. "You're here and you're alive, not kicking just yet but we're off to a good start," he said with a smile.

"Haha, at least you can joke. But seriously, thank you, Sage," she said seriously.

"You're welcome. But now are you going to tell me why you were there?" he asked.

She had been hoping he wouldn't ask.

"I'm a spy, Sage. I've been working for the Omens, leaking information about the Screaming Demons to them. I just didn't have anything to tell them and so they were making me pay for it," she admitted. "Basically, I'm the worst spy and the worst person ever."

Sage looked her over long and hard.

"You need to tell Fiona and Grier," he said.

"How can I tell them, Sage? They could kill me too."

"Don't be so dramatic. They wouldn't do that but you need to tell them. They're the only ones who can keep you safe."

"They wouldn't keep me safe, not after this incident. They'll kick me out," Mia said, "and I'd have nowhere to go."

"You trusted me by telling me the truth, now trust me again when I say that they are not horrible people. They will listen, Mia. Please come with me so we can tell them. They need to know that the Omens are up to something and they need to be prepared."

"No… Alright, I'll tell them when the time is right," she said.

"Of course, I'll be right behind you every step of the way."

"Will you keep it a secret until then?"

"Of course," he said with a smile.

4

―――――――

ia was trapped. Beaten and tortured, all she could do was think about the argument she'd had with Sage and the mistakes she had made as she drifted in and out of consciousness.

*"You did what?" She shouldn't have done it. She should've listened to Sage and just come clean... A lot sooner.*

*"It was just a number." Her tears were pouring out and her mascara started to run. She made no effort to correct that.*

*"I thought I could trust you." Sage couldn't even look at her at that moment.*

*"They said... Tyler said he just needed something... anything..."*

*"And?"*

*"And I'll be free from the Omens, forever... all my debts... erased."*

*Sage sighed. "And you believed him?"*

Mia was stupid enough to believe the Omens, believe Tyler Sedotal. All he needed was one single piece of information. Give them something… anything… Maybe something real, not fake so they wouldn't accuse her of lying, something so vague that there was no way they could get anything out of it. The Omens were a bunch of idiots.

So she gave them the number Sage called to arrange Fiona's flight. There was no way they would find out anything from a number, right? She was wrong. Dead wrong. The Omens not only found out Fiona's flight plan from the number she provided, they took her, embarrassed her and tortured her.

Not only had Mia betrayed Sage's trust by spying on his phone when he was in the shower, she betrayed Fiona, Grier, the Demons.

She tried to fix it. She wanted to make everything right. It was by luck that the very limited information she knew led the Omens to Fiona. The Demons had to understand that her true loyalty lay with them, not the Omens. She'd made her choice long ago to stay with the Demons. But she still owed the Omens and she had to clear her debt and make a clean exit, cut them out once and for all. That was the right thing to do, at least that's what she had thought.

Hamilton's death though wasn't completely her fault. She didn't mean to hit him. She had to. Dick, Sedotal's second, pointed his gun at her and signaled for her to do something. She knew what kind of person Dick was and that he'd shoot her without hesitation if she didn't do anything. At that moment, she chose her own life and Hamilton paid the price.

Soon enough, she realized that she had chosen wrong. She should have known there was no way the Omens would let her off so easy. Being tortured by the Omens was ten times worse than having a quick death. A shot in the head and be done with it. Mia closed her eyes and images of her torment flashed through her eyes. Could she ever forget what the Omens did to her? She was beaten, raped, shot and left to die. She should've picked death when there was a choice.

Just as she was drifting off again, the sound of a loud crash and gunfire suddenly snapped her back into a moment of lucidity and she realized someone had come for her—the last person in the world she had expected.

She laughed at the thought of being saved by Fiona. Doesn't God have a very twisted way of fucking with people's lives? Mia was never religious. She tried when she was a little girl to please her parents by going to church every week and doing what a good Catholic girl was supposed to, but she never truly believed. She had never asked God for anything in her life. But now, lying and shivering in a pool of her own blood, all she wanted was a quick death.

"God! Can you please hurry the fuck up?!" Her voice was weak and shaky but that was exactly what had led Fiona to her.

"Over here, Grier!" shouted Fiona.

"Fi… o… na…" Mia couldn't help thinking God must be a woman.

* * *

"I MADE a deal with the Omens that I would be their spy, and I was sent in to try to infiltrate the Screaming Demons so I could pass on any information," Mia said.

"So what do they know?" Fiona asked.

"Just the number… the one Sage called to arrange your flight."

"I nearly died…"

"I'm sor…" Mia would say that a million times, or more.

"Hamilton died because of you." Fiona wanted someone to blame for Hamilton's death.

"Fiona, they had a gun pointing at her," Sage moved closer to Mia, just in case… Fiona was the kind of woman who would shoot first and explain later.

"I'm sorry… I should've let them kill me instead…" Mia took the courage to say what she was thinking.

"Maybe you should!"

Grier shot Fiona a look, signaling her to let Mia finish what she had to say.

"What… what they did to me at the warehouse… that was worse than death," Mia continued. The room went quiet for a few seconds.

"I know," Fiona sighed and gave Mia a look, as if to say she knew exactly what she'd gone through.

"Can we trust her?" Grier asked Sage.

"Yes," Sage replied.

"Okay, we'll need some time to go over things. We can respect that you tried to make things right with us, but it still doesn't change the fact that you betrayed us." Grier said as Sage nodded in agreement with him. "We haven't seen or heard anything about the Omens recently, but that doesn't mean they're gone. They will still be looking for you. You need to lay low for now," Grier said.

Once Mia had explained everything to Grier and Fiona, Sage could tell she was a bit shaken up.

"Here," he said as he helped her into one of the rooms at the clubhouse. "Let's get you fixed."

---

## 5

Sage could tell that Mia was frustrated about her current arrangement. It was understandable that Fiona wanted her to lay low. The Demons didn't know how many Omens were still out there and if they would want blood for killing their leader Sedotal. Mia was their only contact in the Demons until she betrayed them and no one in the biker world would forgive a traitor. And even though Fiona may not trust Mia completely, she didn't want Mia to be in danger, especially after what she'd just been through.

For the last few months, Mia did exactly what Fiona told her. She stayed at one of the Demons' properties, which she later learned was Eliana's old house. She hadn't been seen by anyone, not even the neighbors. Sage would run errands and get whatever she needed for her. The doctor would come in every few weeks to check on her. Her last appointment was rather promising, and Mia couldn't wait until she could finally go out in the open and take in some fresh air.

"Let's go for a ride," Sage said with a big grin on his face.

"What...?" Mia said, puzzled. Her wide eyes looking at Sage as if he'd just told a lie.

"You mean... out of the house?" She just needed to make sure she had heard it right.

"Yes, silly, the doc said you're fine to go out and Fiona has agreed to discuss your return to the bar."

Mia screamed at the top of her lungs, sprinted across the living room and hugged Sage.

"Ready?" He passed her a helmet.

Mia took the helmet and gladly put it on. Once Sage had taken his place on the bike, she got on behind him and wrapped herself around him, holding on tight. All the time she'd been working for the bikers, the funny thing was, Mia had never actually been on the back of a bike before and although she was terrified she trusted Sage with her life. Literally.

As they drove off, Mia took in the feeling she got while she was on the bike. Although the initial take-off had been rather frightening, she enjoyed the feeling she got in the pit of her stomach. She could compare it to when a flight takes off or when you leave the platform on a roller coaster ride. She felt free in more ways than one. She could feel the knot that had been in her stomach for a while finally give way and she began to breathe easily.

She had come clean to Fiona and Grier and although her future with the Hell Kats hung in the balance, she was relieved she could now be honest with those around her.

Sage decided to take her out of the city so she could get her head cleared. After the night she had had, he could only imagine what she was going through. Mia took in the scenery as they drove through the city. She watched as the night enveloped the city in darkness and buildings started to light up in every direction. The more Sage drove and the further out they got, the less she could see of the buildings.

He drove alongside a mountain, weaving higher and higher, and he continued to drive until he reached the top where they arrived at a dead end. This was the perfect place to come and look out over the city. It was beautiful at night, when the lights from buildings were lit up and it looked like something out of a movie.

"I don't know what I would've done if it weren't for you," she said to Sage again once they had hopped off the bike and walked over to the side railing that ran along the side of the mountain.

She looked over the city, completely captivated by

the beauty of it all. She felt freer now that she was out of the city.

Mia started to open up to Sage about her life. The stress of everything had been building up for so long that she had just needed someone to listen to her. She had never told her story to anyone before but she trusted Sage and she knew that he would not judge her because of her past.

"My parents believed that worshipping God was the only important thing in life, that and getting married to someone who had the same beliefs," she began.

"I'd never really been able to love God, it's not that I didn't try because I did. I really tried to please my parents for a while by going to a Catholic church and meeting boys who they would approve of. It's just after a while, I couldn't help who I really was anymore. I couldn't be boxed in and I couldn't be tied down to anything or anyone that couldn't see me for who I really was. My one release had always been art. I loved art, I loved it so much it often consumed me. I would go days on end locked up in my room just painting, living off of basically nothing. I couldn't deny myself of something I really wanted to do but my parents did. They denied me over and over again because they couldn't understand why I would waste my life on something that wasn't productive, something that didn't include God. I just couldn't take it anymore. I mean, who wants to be with a family that doesn't accept you? I know I didn't and I know most people would agree with me. And so I took it upon myself to leave, I had to get out! I couldn't stay there any longer or who knows what I would've done. But I guess leaving didn't turn out that great," she said sounding overwhelmed with emotions. She let out a small laugh when she mentioned how her life had turned out.

Sage hadn't said anything, he didn't need to go into his story. His life story was his own and he couldn't bring himself to share it with anyone, especially Afghanistan. That had been the worst time of his life. So he stood next to her staring out into the city and continued to listen.

"When you're 16 and a runaway, it is extremely easy to fall into the wrong crowd like I did. It seems to be a pattern in my life," she said with sadness in her eyes.

Sage just wanted to hold her and make her feel safe. She had been damaged for so long he could see her emotional scars starting to show on her face as if they were physical wounds. He could never fully understand her pain but he wished he could take it away.

"I was so desperate to make it on my own, to prove my parents wrong, to show them that I could be an artist that I had to take anything I could get. Whatever job opportunity popped up, I had to take it. That's when I got into drugs. At first, I was only selling them but after hanging with the wrong crowd for so long it was hard not to join in and eventually I did. The first drug I ever used was cocaine. I wouldn't say I got addicted to it as fast as most people. For some reason, I had to take a lot of it to get high and so I switched it up. I started taking the harder drugs because go big or go home, right? Looking back now, I should've just gone home after all. But I was young and naive, convinced that I could do just about anything and still make it out alive." She took a moment to catch her breath, the memory of her past weighing heavily on her chest.

She had been looking out into the city, watching her life on repeat as if someone had put it on as a movie.

"I remember the day I almost died like it was yesterday. It had been a couple of years since I left home, still not an artist and constantly in a state of self-hatred. Why had I left home? What was the point of it when I still hadn't done what I had set out to do? I didn't even try hard to get into the art world which I obviously know was my fault. I had disappointed myself more than I could have disappointed my family. I'd become so heavily addicted to drugs, I had become a low life, the lowest of the low. I was fortunate enough to have never had to beg for food, I had always made it by but I was homeless, living on the streets with other kids just like me. And I say kids because back then I was just a kid. I remember I had taken a mixture of different things, trying to get as high as possible so I could forget about the life I always dreamed of having that had begun to feel so far out of reach. I closed my eyes for what felt like a second so I could let the drugs take over my mind and my senses and the next thing I knew I woke up in a hospital bed. My parents were never notified and I'm sure they think I'm dead. I still can't remember many of the details of that day, I had been so out of it, but it was ever since then that I decided I had to stop using drugs. My life was still never easy, it took me a while to get off of the streets and I suppose my life got a different kind of messy after that," she said.

"You're a survivor," he said once she had fallen silent.

She looked up at him with her beautiful brown eyes and smiled.

Sage couldn't help thinking that even now, with her life story before him, she was still so beautiful. She had shown so much perseverance and strength that he knew that she could get through whatever life threw at her even if she didn't believe it herself.

It was becoming harder for him not to fall for her. He had never wanted her so bad.

## 6

Mia felt so alone after the battle with the Omens. The Demons didn't trust her, and rightfully so. Hamilton was dead and they blamed her. To be fair it wasn't completely her fault, but she knew they had the right to be angry. If she were completely honest, she was sorry and she wished that she was the one who had died instead.

Everything worked out though. For now. Tyler Sedotal was dead and he deserved it. He was responsible for her suffering and he was stupid enough to attack Grier and Fiona at their house. He had been such a horrible man, trying to claim things that hadn't belonged to him. He deserved to die. Mia was glad that he had. It finally gave her a reason to leave the Omens; no one wanted her there anyway. She had finally gotten out of one of the biggest mistakes of her life and yet she was still so alone. Soon enough she'd have completely no one. She was sure that if she were kicked out of the Screaming Demons, she would lose Sage too.

The Hell Kats didn't want her around either. The Hell Kats had stopped talking to her, made her feel like an outcast and yet she wanted to be one of them so badly. While she was still on their good side she had felt so at home with them. They were always nice to her and they involved her in almost everything; she wanted to stay a Hell Kat. She knew she had messed up and messed up badly but she had tried to prove her loyalty, and there was nothing else she could do. She could only hope that they would forgive her. She knew it would take time and she understood that but she needed to belong again. It had been a while since she had last heard from Fiona and so she decided that she had to take care of herself. She felt that the best thing for her to do would be to leave town. She had nothing keeping her here, well, besides Sage, but he had made it clear that nothing would ever happen between them.

She could make it somewhere new, somewhere where no one knew her. That could be the best thing for her. She had nowhere else to turn if she stayed. She had no family, no friends and she had pretty much cut any ties she had. Maybe she could start over, finally become the artist she had always set out to be when she had left home at 16. She could finally get the dream she had always wanted. That could be worth a new beginning, that could be worth leaving everyone and everything behind.

"Sage, hey. It's me," she said when he picked up her call on the second ring.

"Hey, what's going on?" She knew he could already sense something was up in her voice. She had tried to hide it but clearly, she had failed. She had tried to practice her speech before she called him but just hearing his voice had her come undone.

"I need to leave town. I have no one anymore and I have nowhere to go while I stay here. No one wants me around which is understandable but I can't take it. I need to get out. I feel so alone, it would just make sense for me to leave and start over somewhere else," she said.

"Calm down," he said. "Meet me at the bar in 10 minutes so we can talk about this face to face," he said just before hanging up, not waiting for a reply.

Mia can't say no. She wanted to see him one last time before she left, she had to say goodbye to him properly after everything he had done for her. He had saved her life one too many times and he deserved a proper goodbye. She just wished she had had the chance to kiss him, she wished she could've been something more to him. She could've made him happy if he had let her. She knew she had always flirted with him but it had always been more than that to her, she just couldn't show it.

The rejection from him always stung. He clearly didn't see her as anything more than a friend, she thought.

Mia had taken a seat at the bar patiently waiting for Sage to get there. No one would talk to her but she knew they were all staring at her, discussing among themselves. 'How she can walk into the bar like that after everything that she's done' they'd be saying. She had to leave soon, she could not stand being here any longer. She let her mind wander while she sat there waiting, trying to distract herself from the Screaming Demons and Hell Kats that were talking about her.

She had started to picture a life with Sage, a happy life somewhere far away from this place, away from all the drama that followed her. They could live somewhere out of the city, with two kids playing in the garden while she and Sage sat on their patio watching and laughing. She sighed at the thought. It would've been nice if things were different, she thought to herself.

"You don't have to leave," Sage said as he came up behind her and joined her at the bar.

He called the bartender over and ordered them a drink each, a whiskey neat for him and a vodka soda for her. He would definitely need a drink if he were to talk Mia out of leaving. He could not bear the thought of her not being around, being her annoying self.

"You're joking. Of course, I do. No one wants me here, Sage," she said. "And I honestly don't blame them. I have literally messed up everything for everyone, especially myself. I'm just bad news," she admitted. No one could deny that she was telling the truth but Sage had to fight for her to stay. He would've fought Grier and now he would have to fight Mia.

The bar was pretty empty so the bartender didn't waste much time making their drinks and soon their drinks were placed in front of them. Mia took hers and had a few sips, hoping it would calm her down a bit. She felt on edge with the talk of leaving town.

"That's only because everything is still so fresh, Mia, literally everything just happened and everyone is coming to terms with it. They all need time to come to terms with the role you played in it too. Yes, you may have been working for the Omens but when you think about it, your heart has always been with the Demons. They might not see that right now, but I'm sure they'll eventually get over the feeling that you are a traitor," he said as he too took a sip of his drink.

"You can tell by their faces they never will. They hate me," she said as she hung her head.

"Yes, they'll hate you, or should I say they'll dislike you. Hate is a very strong word, but they'll get over it they just need time. You running away will not help anything, Mia. What good would it do to you or to anyone else?" he asked. Mia took another sip of her drink as she thought about that.

"It would get me out of this situation. Even if it's a temporary fix at least I won't be here under everyone's eyes. They look at me like I'm scum," she sighed. "I could start a new life somewhere, somewhere where no one knows me and I could finally make the right decisions in life. I could go to art school and learn how to paint properly. I could get a proper job that doesn't involve any underneath the table dealings of any sort. I told you I'm bad news but I feel like now would be a good time to start fresh."

They both sat there in silence while they finished their drinks. Sage finished his before her and waited for her to finish as well.

"Come on, let's go," Sage demanded as he got up from his seat.

"Where are we going?" Mia asked.

"We're going to Fiona. She can help you, Mia," he said as he left money on the bar and led her to Fiona who was in the offices at the bar.

Mia knew Sage had a point, that Fiona could help her, but she couldn't stop herself from being absolutely terrified of seeing her. Fiona probably hated Mia just as much as everyone else, if not more. Because of Mia, she had lost her best friend; Fiona had every right to hate Mia. Mia had almost lost her family business, she knew that was important to Fiona. Her dad had left it to her when he had passed, and she and Grier had worked hard to make it their own.

In spite of her fear of Fiona, as they walked toward her office, Mia had convinced herself that although she was set on leaving town, she didn't want to lose her association with the Hell Kats. She still wanted to be one of them - the trouble was how she'd find the words and the courage to say that to Fiona.

"Come in," Fiona called when Sage knocked on her door.

Sage led the way while Mia trailed in after him like a puppy with its tail between its legs.

She honestly just wanted to turn around and go back out of the door the minute she saw Fiona.

"Ahh, Mia, what can I do for you?" She asked. "Come to get some information?" she joked.

It made Mia uncomfortable; obviously, that was the point. Mia wanted to be anywhere other than where she was. She wished a sinkhole would open up under her and swallow her whole. It was the least she deserved.

"Fiona, I cannot tell you how sorry I am about the mess I have caused, truly I am so sorry for everything and although I had thought it would be best for me to leave town, Sage has convinced me to stay. I would really love to stay a Hell Kat. I've felt at home for the first time in a long time," she pleaded.

"How can we trust you? " Fiona asked, "after every-thing you have done?"

"I would do anything to prove to you that you can trust me again. I've got nothing left. All I've ever wanted was to live my life but I always found my way into the wrong group. I'm done with that. I feel like the Hell Kats is where I need to be, I feel that if I belonged here again, I could do anything in life. I want to be an artist, it has been my dream for the longest time and I just want to be a loyal Hell Kat." Mia could feel a burning sensation in her chest as she spoke of finally working on her dream, she felt passion ignite inside her. She knew Sage had been right about her needing to see Fiona. She didn't want to make it anywhere more than she wanted to make it within the Hell Kats.

"So you want to leave town and become an artist?" Fiona asked. She looked at Mia with a raised eyebrow.

"Yes, my only chance of doing anything would be to start fresh, where no one would know me but I want to stay with the Hell Kats," she said.

"Despite my best interest and possibly the interest of the Screaming Demons, I like you. You had a way when you worked as a Hell Kat, and don't think we didn't know about you not pleasing anybody because we've known the whole time but you show a lot of fire and I like that but I still don't know if I can trust you," Fiona said.

"Please, Fiona, I'll do anything to prove my loyalty." Mia couldn't walk away from this without a fight. She felt like the Hell Kats were her family. She hadn't known anyone knew about her not sleeping with anyone. She had thought she was getting away with it because no one had said anything to her about it before. Clearly, they weren't that mad about it though if Fiona just complimented her.

"There is something in Florida you could help with," Fiona said after a long time.

"Yes, anything. I'll do anything," Mia said as she hung on to Fiona's every word.

"You'll need to help clean up the mess that is the Omens. There are a few of them still trying to overrun us in the city and they need to leave," Fiona said. "You'd need to expand our club. Everyone must know that the Screaming Demons will never back down and that we are here to stay," Fiona said.

"I'll do it if it can prove my loyalty is to you and the Screaming Demons, I'll do it," Mia said.

Fiona smiled at that. "That's what I like to hear," she said. "You will leave today."

## 7

"Mia, you can leave now. I'd like to talk to Sage alone," Fiona said.

"No problem, I'll wait for you outside," she said to Sage.

"Alright," he said, not looking back at her as she left.

Mia turned and left the room. Once the door closed behind her, Fiona turned to Sage.

"I need you to go with her," she said matter of factly.

"What? But my job is here," he says. He can't believe she is doing this to him. It wasn't his job to play babysitter. He did not sign up for this.

"Yes, but I need you to do this for me. It is very important that nothing goes wrong with this," Fiona said. She looked at him as a mother would look at a child, very stern and extremely powerful.

"I understand that but surely there will be people in

Florida who could do that," Sage argued. "I'm not a babysitter."

"Please don't fight me on this, Sage. I trust you and I know you will do anything to make sure nothing turns sour. I will not send Mia without you," Fiona said. She proceeded to stare him down. Sage had to agree, he knew there was no getting out of it.

Fiona really knew how to press his buttons. She knew Sage would want Mia to get out safely and that he would do what was needed to make it happen.

"You're doing this on purpose," he said.

"I have no idea what you're talking about, Sage," she said with a smile, "I just need you to make sure Mia gets the job done."

"Hmm," Sage said with a knowing look. "Sure you do. Well, I suppose you know I can't say no."

"That's what I like to hear," Fiona said with a clap of her hands. "Now get going, she won't wait forever, " she said while waving him out.

Sage always knew his boss had been keeping an eye on him but he had never realized that she had seen him express any of his feelings toward Mia. He may have never said anything to anyone about how he felt when he was around her but clearly people could pick up on it without him even knowing. He had clearly messed up. How could he be alone with Mia for a few days, holed up in hotel rooms together? It sounded like a disaster waiting to happen. His feelings for Mia had continued to grow the more he was around her. He wouldn't be able to stop himself and knew what Mia was like. She had always been the flirty one out of the two of them and he could only imagine what she would be like when it was just the two of them, no one for him to turn to when she became too much.

He walked out of the building to find Mia standing, waiting patiently by his bike.

"I'll drop you off at your place so you can pack a small bag of clothes. We have limited space on the bike, and then I'll come pick you up in 20 minutes," he said while handing her the spare helmet.

"Okay... So we're going down to Florida together?" she asked.

"Yes, we are," he replied. The trip down was going to be torture. He knew they'd have to make a few stops along the way and he could only imagine what would happen if he let his guard down.

Don't let your guard down then, he said to himself.

If only it were that easy. He didn't know how much longer he could go on denying her.

He dropped Mia off and headed home to pack a small bag for himself. Soon enough he was packed and on his way to Mia.

"I'm outside," he sent her a text message.

"Coming," she replied.

Once their bags were placed securely in the panniers on his bike, Sage and Mia headed out of town.

It had just gone noon when they left so Sage knew they'd only get a few hours of the ride in before they'd have to stop off somewhere for the night. He tried not to think about it.

As he drove he tried to focus on their surroundings, noting the signs they drove past and the things he would see along the way. The scenery was mostly just road and glass but the sky was a beautiful color above them. He tried not to focus on Mia's body pressing up against his and her hands around his waist. Not long now, he thought.

He continued to focus on the road. He started counting the bikes that could pass him just to try to keep his mind busy.

One... two... three... four... five... he thought. He was just about ready to lose his mind.

Just as the dark started to come down on them, Sage pulled up to a hotel just off the road.

It was a small hotel that only consisted of three stories. It had a parking lot just off the front near the reception and continued to go into a bit of a circle as the beige buildings began. Sage couldn't complain though. It may not be much but it would get them off the road and Mia would have to let go of Sage. He'd be truly grateful for that.

"We will rest here for the night and continue tomor-row," he said while hopping off the bike. Mia followed suit and grabbed the bags from the panniers on the back of the bike.

"I'll go ahead and get us some rooms, just wait here for me, I shouldn't be long," he said. Mia nodded and stayed where she was and he headed inside.

Sage headed to the reception to get rooms for them, deciding it would be better if they got separate rooms. He knew that it would be a really big mistake if they were to share a room.

"Good evening," he said as he greeted the young man behind the reception desk, "I'd like two rooms for the night, please."

"Hello, sir. Unfortunately, we only have one room available. We could organize separate beds if that would help?" the young man asked.

"I guess that will do," Sage said as the young man handed him the room key.

"It will just take about 5 minutes, sir, but in the meantime let me get someone to take your bags up and you can go check out our restaurant," the young man said. Sage handed over his bag and pointed Mia out to the young man so he knew her bag needed to be taken too.

Sage headed back to Mia and explained to her that they'd have to wait a bit for the room.

"That's alright," she said. "I'm getting rather hungry come to think of it, so let's go check the restaurant out like he suggested," she said as she already started heading in its direction.

Once in the restaurant, they both ordered something to eat and a drink each. It had been a long trip and they both needed something to calm their minds. Sage wasn't the only one getting ideas about them being alone together. They ate their dinner in silence and slowly finished their drinks, the trip taking its toll on both of them. Once they had both finally finished their drinks, Sage got the bill, paid and they both headed up to their room.

They walked into an entrance hall that had a staircase hugging the wall on the left. They continued to walk up two flights of stairs, down a corridor, passing a few other rooms, and finally, they arrived at their room, number 19. The tension between the two of them during the walk had escalated. For the first time since they had met, they would be alone and the thought was rather scary for both of them.

Sage was extremely grateful when he saw the separate beds. Although they might be stuck in the same room together, at least he wouldn't have to go through the torture of sharing a bed with her. He didn't think he would be strong enough to keep his hands to himself like he had the last time they shared his bed. It had been by luck that she had fallen asleep then. He doubted if either of them would sleep this time. Sage wasn't sure if Mia had been thinking the same thing though, was she disappointed when she saw the separate beds? He didn't know, she didn't give anything away.

"I'm going to have a quick shower to get the trip off of me," Mia said as she grabbed her things and headed to the bathroom. Sage couldn't stop himself from picturing her naked in the shower, with water dripping down her body and steam radiating off of her.

Get control of yourself, you have to keep your distance and thinking like this won't help, he thought to himself.

Mia reentered the room in fresh clothes. He could smell her sickeningly sweet body wash coming off of her skin. It reminded him of vanilla and caramel. If her body was covered in the literal thing he would've started licking it off by now.

Stop it, Sage, you're getting ahead of yourself, he thought.

It didn't help that he could tell she was no longer wearing a bra, her nipples just slightly peaking through her thin top. Her hair, wet just touching her shoulders, and her face had been washed clean of any makeup - she looked breathtaking. He should've left, he should've gone outside for fresh air. He should've but he didn't, he just continued to stare at her in all her beautiful glory.

Mia saw Sage had been staring at her since she had come out of the bathroom.

"How can I help you?" she said to him teasingly, flirting with him like she always had back at the bar. Sage should've moved, he should've headed for the bathroom so he could also take a shower. A shower definitely would've helped clear his mind and it would've given him a bit of privacy to sort himself out.

She walked over to him and shyly put a hand on his chest, his breathing quickened.

Sage, man, walk away. Take your eyes off of her and walk out of this room, he yelled internally.

He knew he should stop her before anything happened but he couldn't focus on anything but her hand on his chest and the look of lust and desire that had begun to grow in her eyes.

She slowly started to reach up and placed a hand behind his head, working her fingers into his hair. He closed his eyes as he allowed himself to give in.

Within a second Mia had leaned forward and closed her mouth on his. Shocked his eyes flew open; hers, however, were closed. He looked at her fluttering eyelids, counted a few of the freckles on the bridge of her nose, and noticed how she had a freckle just above her eyelashes on the lid of her eyes.

He gave in, he couldn't resist her anymore. He closed

his eyes and savored the moment. He would never want to forget this.

He wrapped his arms around her as both of her arms wrapped around his neck.

Her body felt so warm and soft against his. He wanted this, he wanted it so badly but he knew it was wrong. It was so wrong and yet it felt too damn good.

He moaned against her soft lips.

He gently opened her mouth with his tongue, and she didn't fight it. He picked her up and pushed her against one of the walls, kissing down her neck while she wrapped her legs around his waist.

He could hear her breathing quicken, and a small moan escaped her lips. He was so ready to take her to bed and rip every item of clothing off of her body. He was ready to lick her and kiss her like she was covered in caramel.

Sage so badly wanted to take it further but the part of his brain that had been telling him to resist kicked in and he had to put a stop to it before anything more happened. With one final kiss, he moved off of the wall, lowering Mia back onto her feet. He ran his hands through her hair, she sighed with her eyes still closed. He dropped his hand to his side, her eyes flew open. She knew something had changed. Her eyes were wide, staring at him, questioningly.

"We can't do this," he said as he finally pulled himself

away from her. He walked across the room to create some distance between the two of them. He almost left the room this time.

"Are you fucking kidding me? What the hell is the matter with you?" she yelled. He could tell that if there were objects near her she would've started throwing them at him. He wouldn't blame her if she did.

"I'm here to watch over you, to protect you. It is not in my job description to have sex with you," he said as he proceeded to go to the bed at the far side of the room, lay down and roll over so he was no longer looking at her. He could see the hurt and anger in her eyes and he couldn't stand to see it.

"You're an asshole," she said as she climbed into the empty bed and switched off the lights.

She may think he was an asshole but he was truly trying to look out for her. He didn't want to do anything while they were in that position just for her to regret it later.

Mia couldn't deny that she wanted Sage more than ever after their kiss the previous night. It had been so overwhelming and so heated. She could still feel his lips against hers even after she had woken up.

It had taken her a long time to finally fall asleep after their make-out session. She still couldn't believe that it had happened. She had wanted to kiss Sage for so long now that she was starting to think she would never get the chance. And technically he started it, maybe she had been a little too forward with her pajama choice, she knew full well how revealing her top was. She had just meant to tease him. She had no idea it would go as far as it did. She loved every single second of it though. The way his body reacted to hers just meant that he also felt something for her, he wanted her just as badly as she wanted him.

She just wanted to rip Sage's clothes off and have her way with him but he had stopped it before it could go that far.

She had to make him change his mind. She understood that he was there to protect her, his little line last night had just irritated her

*"It's not in my job description to have sex with you," he had said.*

Yes, she knew that but that doesn't change the fact that they both wanted each other.

"Go put your things in the pannier while I go pay for the room. We need to head out again," he said as he walked out of the room. He hadn't paid Mia much attention and it had started to annoy her. He clearly wanted to push her away now, she thought, make her give up, but that would not happen. She wanted him and she would stop at nothing to have him. She knew that.

"Okay," she said as she walked passed him to get to the bike. If he wanted to play hard to get, she would do the same thing.

Two can play that game she thought.

She waited patiently while he took care of the bill and as she waited she came up with a plan. She would torture him all day until he had no choice and caved. She knew he wanted her. He could not deny that after what had happened the night before. If he tried to deny it she knew he would be lying.

Once he was on the bike, Mia got on and pressed her body against his, wrapping her arms around his torso as tightly as she could and resting her head against his. She knew he wouldn't be able to resist. He couldn't resist her body last night so she knew she could wear him down if she tried hard enough. However, he took no notice as he got the bike going and pulled out of the parking lot. He didn't react at all. Mia could sense she had a hard day ahead of her.

After a while, Mia's body ached from sitting on the bike for so long and from holding on so tightly and she proceeded to loosen her grip to try to alleviate some of the pain. Her body hadn't been the same since the attack. Her body constantly ached for no apparent reason - she hated it. She used to take her body for granted before. She had put it through so much, especially when she was still doing drugs. Now she wished she could go back and change everything. She was only 25 and yet she felt like she was 40 something with all her body aches.

Every couple of hours Sage would pull into a garage so they could stretch, get something to eat and fill up the tank. Mia was extremely grateful for that and whenever she stretched, she made sure that her shirt lifted, exposing some of her skin so Sage could see. She wanted him to watch her, to crave her. She wanted him to want her just as much as she wanted him. She wasn't usually the type to tease men but she had with Sage. After all, he wasn't just some man. It was Sage and she always got what she wanted.

She thought for sure that this was the way to get him, but he had hardly looked in her direction since they left the hotel. He really was trying to ignore her. Mia knew she was coming off as desperate but she didn't care. She had never wanted anyone as badly as she wanted him. She had to break through his guard if she were going to succeed.

After trying and failing to get his attention, Sage pulled into a hotel as it had started getting dark.

This hotel was quite similar to the last one, Mia thought, clearly it was a franchise.

"You wait here while I go get the key," he said as he got off the bike.

Mia was hopeful when he said key instead of keys. Could that mean that her plan had worked after all, she thought to herself. She hoped that if they shared a room again tonight that instead of two beds there would be one. She knew Sage was a gentleman but she would not let him sleep on the floor so he would have to join her in bed.

She stood by the bike waiting patiently for Sage to get back, the temperature had started dropping and she just wanted to get into a warm bed after the long drive.

Her muscles ached, her ass hurt like a bitch and she would rather be laying flat for a while instead of having to stand. She was just about ready to start heading to the reception to see what was going on when Sage walked out of the front doors.

Mia watched as Sage walked up to her. She couldn't help but stare as his body moved. He walked with the grace of someone who demanded to be seen. People could not help but notice if he walked into a room. Mia couldn't take her eyes off of him. She wanted his strong arms wrapped around her again, she wanted his hands all over her body. She was so desperate for him.

"Let's go get dinner before we head up," he said, "I'm starving."

"What about our bags?" Mia asked.

"Just leave them in the pannier and we'll collect them once we're done," he said with a smile.

It seemed as though his mood had done a complete 360. He had not smiled once the entire trip.

"Alright, let's go eat," she said.

Mia followed him to the restaurant, they took a seat at a table, looked at the menu and placed their orders.

"How did you find the trip today?" Sage asked her.

"It wasn't too bad but my body is aching everywhere. I guess my body will never be the same after... well, you know" she said with a little laugh. "And how did you find it?"

"Oh, not too bad. I had you to keep me warm whenever the wind got a bit much," he said with a wink.

Mia thought his mood to be extremely strange. He had ignored her all day and all of a sudden he was flirting with her. It didn't make any sense. She became so confused that she couldn't even register a flirty comment to say back. He had clearly caught on to her though with his little comment and yet had done nothing all day. Did he not want her anymore, she thought to herself.

He couldn't have faked his desire for her last night. That was real and Mia knew it.

Soon their food arrived and the conversation died out a bit. She kept looking at him questioningly during dinner and he just smiled back at her.

Strange, she thought.

"How's your food?" he asked halfway through dinner.

Mia had ordered pasta, one of her favorite dishes, spaghetti bolognese to be exact.

"It's delicious," she replied as she finished the mouthful she had put in her mouth the minute he asked, "and how is your steak?" she asked him. Sage had ordered a medium-rare steak with potato chips.

"Just wonderful," he said as he licked some of the pepper sauce from the corner of his mouth.

Mia had to stop looking at his mouth. He seemed to be taunting her. Constantly licking his lips, drawing her attention to his mouth was trouble.

After dinner, they made their way back to the bike and got their bags in silence. Mia had to keep her head down because watching Sage had started to do things to her and soon she would have to hurl her body onto his.

Mia turned around after grabbing her bag so she could ask Sage where the room was when she was almost knocked over by him because he was standing so close to her. She didn't see it coming.

He was so close Mia could smell the whiskey he had during dinner coming off his breath.

He leaned in closer and just when Mia thought he was about to kiss her again, just when she began to think her plan had worked, he handed her a room key.

"Here is your room key," he said with yet another wink. And just like that, he had started heading toward his own room.

The bastard had got separate rooms this time.

He had won this time but he had no chance, overall; Mia wouldn't stop until he was hers.

9

---

As morning came they headed out early again. Sage wanted to get there as soon as possible as the trip with Mia had started becoming almost unbearable. He knew what she had tried to do the day before, constantly pressing her body against his unnecessarily. The way she stretched was almost spell bounding, the way she would rotate her hips as she bent forward and sighed when she got the perfect stretch was almost intoxicating. Sage had tried not to watch. Always looking out of the corner of his eye, Mia hadn't noticed. She seemed to have gotten more irritated as the day went on.

The physical tension between the two of them had been growing for a rather long time and Sage knew he could not and would not let himself get carried away, especially now since they had to open the new branch.

He had to be professional around Mia even when she made it almost impossible.

Sage had not been with anyone since Laura and he knew that it would be a huge step for him to take regardless of who he took that step with. He had never gotten to say goodbye to her and so he felt like in some way they were still connected; he'd feel as if he were in a way cheating on her. He knew he was stupid to think that way. She wasn't even alive but he had loved her and that had been the hardest trauma for him to get over.

Mia had had enough of being on the bike. She didn't know how much more she could take. Her body had begun to scream at her in pain. She had to try her hardest to keep herself distracted. She tried counting yellows cars but that didn't work because there weren't many yellow cars. She then tried to count the trees as they flew past them but Sage was a fast driver so most of the trees were a blur and she never knew if it was a tree, a bush or maybe even a person on the side of the road.

Resting during the night didn't help because her body just needed to get off the damn bike. She would've much preferred doing the trip in a car. At least then she would've been able to stretch herself out more often in the back seat. She really hoped that this would be the final day of riding.

She was so relieved when they arrived that she almost kissed the ground. If she ever had to get back onto a bike, it would be too soon. And especially with Sage, having to wrap her body around his and feel his chest under her hands for so long had almost begun to feel like torture throughout the trip.

The Screaming Demons in Florida were expecting them; Fiona had already told them about her and Sage. The plans had already begun. The operations had been led by Adam, a Screaming Demon who wanted full control over the situation but bowed down to Mia and Sage when they arrived. Adam was an old friend of Fiona's, always seeking more power and a higher rank within the Screaming Demons.

"You must be Mia and Sage," he said as they got off the parked bike in the parking lot of the Screaming Demons bar.

Fiona had arranged a meeting with Adam for the two of them upon arrival so he could tell them what had happened so far. He knew all the ins and outs of the bar and how things were being run while the Omens were still in Florida.

"Hi, I'm Mia and this is Sage," Mia said as she extended her hand for a quick handshake. Instead, Adam proceeded to shake only Sage's hand. He clearly does not want me here, Mia thought. She, however, brushed it off. It was her operation now and everyone in town should accept it. She could so easily get him out of a job, and he had to know that because there could be no other reason as to why he'd acted like he was superior to her.

Adam was a guy of medium build, with green eyes and dark brown hair.

"So what can you tell us?" she asked, taking note of his attitude toward her. Something will need to be done about that, she thought to herself.

"Well, so far the Omens that remain in town have started to back off. They heard about what happened to Tyler and no one wants to be next."

"That's good. They should be scared," Mia said. After everything she had seen, she knew what the Screaming Demons were capable of. And if she were in anyone else's shoes, specifically the Omens, she would've been terrified.

"Where are the Omens situated?" Sage asked.

"They have a few bars further into the city," Adam said as he turned his head to look in the city's direction.

"So you don't know if any attacks are being planned to fight back against the Screaming Demons?" Sage asked.

"None that I've heard of and I hear a lot," he said to Sage.

"That's brilliant," Mia said. She knew Grier and Fiona would be happy about that.

"It definitely is. But we should always be prepared;

anything can happen when it comes to the Omens," Adam said.

Both Sage and Mia nodded, they both knew very well that the Omens were very unexpected sometimes but they both hoped that because of what had happened to Tyler, no one was out there planning anything.

"Let me make a phone call to Fiona to let her know that we have arrived and to pass on the information. I think she'll be pleased," Mia said.

She walked away and let Adam and Sage talk some more.

Mia dialed Fiona's number and on the third ring she picked up.

"Hello?" she said.

"Hi, Fiona, its Mia."

"Oh, Mia, I've been expecting your call. How was the trip down to Florida?" she asked.

"It was fine. I don't think I'll ever want to ride a bike again though," she said with a chuckle.

"I'm sure it was hard on the body."

"It was, very much so. But I just called to tell you that we have arrived and we're currently here with Adam."

"Perfect," Fiona said, "what has he told you?"

"He's told us that the Omens around here have stopped messing with the Screaming Demons in the area," Mia said.

"That's excellent news, but we have to stay on top of

the game. We can't risk anything just because we think they have backed off," Fiona said.

"Yes, both Sage and I agree with that. I think it's still possible to take over Florida completely Fiona."

"Hmm I think you are right, what do you suggest we do?" Fiona asked.

"Well, I think we need to get rid of the Omens here, once and for all. Run them out of town. Messing with the Screaming Demons comes with a heavy debt," Mia said. And she knew that for sure.

"I like that idea. We need to prove that no one and nothing can stand in our way."

"Yes, and then we take over the bars, turn them into Screaming Demons bars instead so no trace of the Omens is left."

"Excellent idea, Mia!" Fiona said. Mia could hear the excitement in her voice.

## 10

Once Mia was off the phone, Sage took her to the bar the Screaming Demons had called their own. Fiona had told him that they had to go there the minute they arrived so everyone could see who was in charge.

The bar looked similar to the bar back home, Sage thought. It was slightly smaller but nevertheless, it was a nice reminder of home.

"Let's go show them who's boss," Mia said from the entrance. Sage had no idea what she meant but proceeded to follow her inside the bar.

"This is so cool," she said. "It looks almost identical to the one back home," she said with a huge grin plastered on her face.

Sage was surprised to see her so happy. She hadn't been that happy since he had met her.

"I was thinking the same thing!" he said as he too walked into the bar and ordered them drinks. No one knew who they were yet. Besides Adam, no one knew what Sage and Mia looked like.

Mia was so happy to be standing and walking around. She was so happy they had finally made it to Florida, she could literally dance around naked.

Soon she was three drinks in. She was on a bit of a buzz but nothing over the top.

"Come on Sage, let's dance," she said as she grabbed his hand and dragged him to the dance floor.

"Do I even have a choice?" he asked with a laugh. He had also had a few drinks and found it pleasantly surprising. He had never been a big drinker but with Mia being that happy he couldn't help but join in. They started dancing around the booths, and people were laughing and started joining them.

Mia stopped to grab a stool from the bar, which she then proceeded to climb so she could stand on it. Steadying herself, she announced her presence to everyone in the bar.

"Hello everyone!" she yelled. "Can I please get your attention?!"

Everyone stopped what they were doing and stared as she stood there claiming everyone's eyes. Sage thought she looked like she was glowing while she stood up on the stool. Anyone would be stupid not to notice her, even on a normal day she demanded attention just by being her. She always walked with a bit of an attitude and if she wanted something she was always likely to get it. Sage knew that eventually she would claim him.

"Hello, lovely people of the bar," she said with a little giggle.

Everyone cheered and hooted. She had clearly won the attention of the crowd. They loved her.

"None of you know this but I am Mia! And that man over there," she pointed at Sage, "that man is Sage!"

Everyone knew exactly who they were now. They had all known they were coming to town and thanks to Mia they finally had faces to put to the names they were already aware of.

"And tonight we are here to party in celebration of the Screaming Demons!" she continued to yell.

Everyone continued to cheer for her, slowly chanting her name throughout the bar. She had claimed her place.

"Mia! Mia! Mia! Mia!" everyone roared.

"Screaming Demons! Screaming Demons! Screaming Demons! Screaming Demons!" she started yelling back.

"We are here and we will run this place and we will run anyone out of town who does not agree!" she said.

Everyone cheered even more loudly at that statement.

Sage was amazed by her. She was seriously proving herself worthy now, he thought.

Everyone continued to cheer her on as she got down from the stool.

She walked over to where Sage was standing, "Come on, big guy, it's time for a show," she said as she led him to a booth close by.

"Sit down," she demanded, getting extremely confident.

Sage did as he was told and proceeded to sit down at her command. She was feisty tonight and he liked that she was taking control.

Mia had never given a lap dance before but there was something inside of her telling her to do it and she was in such a good mood she couldn't stop herself. She hoped that she would look sexy while doing it instead of stupid because that would be so embarrassing, she thought. Sage had been denying her for so long, and seeing him in a good mood with her just made it easier for her to take the leap and do it. She had never seen herself as sexy. All of her life she had just thought she was pretty average, just another girl with brown eyes and black hair. Guys had obviously cat called her before yelling out 'hey sexy' or 'hey beautiful' but men did that all the time. She never thought it was because they actually thought she was sexy or even beautiful. She hadn't had much luck in relationships either. Actually, she had never had a proper relationship. She didn't expect that from Sage after a lap dance but at the moment she just wanted to be all over him.

Just as Sage sat down she turned around so her back was facing him. Sage was a little confused but doesn't move. She slightly parted her legs, and bent over from her torso, and swept her hand across the floor from one foot to the other, just as she reached the opposite foot she bent at her knees and looked over her shoulder leaning more on her one leg. Sage watched in awe, was she trying to give him a lap dance, he wondered.

She then got up and swiveled around to face him, running her one hand down the one side of her body before she brought her hand back up to her mouth so she could emphasize her mouth when she started biting her bottom lip while she gently swayed from one foot to the other, bending at the knees so her hips moved with a bit of attitude.

God, she's so sexy, Sage thought to himself.

At that stage, the whole bar had stopped to watch her performance. Everyone was completely captivated. She proceeded to slowly lower herself onto his lap, separating her legs over his knees so she was straddling him. She gently brushed her breasts across his face as she slowly started to bend backward. Sage was completely spellbound and shocked. How could her body do that, he asked himself.

Sage started to notice more of the women in the bar

had started to follow her lead, all grabbing a partner and giving them a dirty little lap dance.

Sage brought his attention back to Mia who had made her way back to now facing him again. She got off of him and turned around, so this time when she sat back down her back would be facing him. She opened her legs and grabbed one of his hands and slowly ran it down the middle of her body. Sage's heart rate had begun to pick up. He couldn't deny that he wanted her and he wanted her badly.

Sage grabbed her by the hand and led her back to the office. He couldn't take it anymore. He wanted her and he wanted her right then.

Once in the office, Sage locked the door and then pushed Mia up against the door, wrapping his fingers in her hair. She moaned. She had wanted it so badly since their kiss the other night, she only hoped that this time he wouldn't pull away. She wouldn't be able to bear it if he did.

He didn't.

He gently pulled her head back by tugging at her hair, laying kisses all the way down her neck till he reached her breasts. He tugged at her shirt and she lifted up her arms willingly so he could take it off. Slowly he pulled it up and over her head, throwing it to the far corner of the office.

"Hmm," he moaned as he took a look at her in her

bra. She had freckles splattered across her shoulders and he bent forward to start kissing them, moving from one shoulder to the next. He got to her breasts again and laid soft kisses along her exposed skin. She moaned at his touch.

He brought his hands to her jeans and started to undo them. She followed suit and tugged them off and kicked them to the side. She reached for the trim of his shirt, pulling it over his head and also throwing it into one of the corners in the office. She looked him over, his chest was broad and evenly muscular. She ran her hands over his chest and torso, savoring the feel of his skin under her hands. He pulled back into her, wanting to taste and feel her lips against his again. His hands reached for the back of her bra, quickly undoing it so her upper body was completely exposed. He opened his mouth and she opened hers, and soon their tongues were connecting and she had started tugging at his pants, pulling the zipper down.

All that could be heard was their heavy breathing and zippers being drawn down.

Sage ran one of his hands down her body, reaching the top of her panties. He started to peel them away, pushing them down her legs while he trailed kisses down the middle of her chest and stomach as his hands worked down her legs. He got to his knees and removed her panties one leg at a time. She moved her body to his command, still overwhelmed that it was finally happening but completely intoxicated with anticipation. Once her panties were thrown into the corner, joining the rest of their clothes, Sage ran his hands up the sides of her legs, stopping as he came to her ass, giving it a gentle squeeze. He started to run kisses along her left hip bone while Mia found her hands in his hair. She couldn't help but moan as she patiently waited for his hands and mouth to explore the rest of her body.

Sage brought his hands forward and ran them up between her legs, stopping just as he got to her sex. He then stood up and moved her to the desk which he cleared by sweeping his hands across it.

"Lay down on your back," he said. Mia happily obeyed his order as she got onto the desk and laid down. As she lay down she could feel the trembling of the desk under her skin as it moved with the base coming from the bar, making her body feel extremely sensitive. Sage moved her body into the position he wanted so her legs were landing over the side of the desk and her ass on the edge. Mia took note of the erection she could see through his boxers.

"Are you not going to take those off?" she asked as she looked at his boxers.

"In time. First, I think I'll have some fun," he replied and with that, he lowered himself onto his knees so he was in between her legs.

Mia had been waiting for this moment for so long that she lost all of her focus in that moment as she focused only on Sage.

She could no longer hear the rattling of bottles that she could hear echoing from the bar earlier. She could also no longer hear the sound of laughter and music. All she could hear was the sound of her heart beating in her ears and her breathing as it quickened. Her body trembled under Sage's touch, her hands gripped the side of the desk, and as soon as Sage had his mouth on her she soon succumbed to the sensation and completely let go.

Sage wanted her and he could no longer keep himself waiting and so within seconds he had her up and bent over the desk, legs apart, waiting. He removed his boxers, quickly grabbed a condom from his discarded jeans, tore through the wrapping and positioned himself behind her. He moved quickly and she gasped in shock as he proceeded to thrust hard and deep in her, grabbing at her waist. He leaned over her, moving his one hand to the back of her head so he could grab a handful of her hair and tug her head back. He bent forward and bit her neck. She moaned, her body completely overwhelmed with pleasure and ecstasy. Sage trailed his hand down her spine as he straightened up and spanked her ass before he finally gave in, soon followed by Mia.

Sage collapsed in a sweaty mess on top of their pile

of clothes, needing a moment to catch his breath which he had almost lost while Mia stayed face down on the desk as she too caught her breath.

"Wow," she said.

Sage laughed. "Yes, 'wow' does seem to fit perfectly."

"That was even better than what I had imagined."

"I could not agree more. I'm literally breathless," Sage said as his breathing had still not gone back to normal.

"Do you think anyone has noticed our absence?" she asked.

"I think anyone who hasn't would be completely clueless," he replied.

Mia chuckled.

Slowly they started putting their clothes back on and once they had both managed to get their breathing back to normal, put back everything they had moved, walked out of the office and back into the bar.

SAGE KNEW INSTANTLY that having sex with Mia had been a bad idea. It had been good in the moment but he shouldn't have allowed himself to get carried away. He had been tasked with taking care of her, to protect her at all costs. He definitely had not been placed with her to fuck her, just like he had told her a couple of nights before. She had just been way too alluring and seductive for him to resist. He couldn't deny that the sex had been amazing, possibly the best sex he had ever had, but it still didn't make up for the fact that he knew it had been wrong. He needed to make sure he kept his distance. He couldn't risk it happening again although he knew he secretly wouldn't mind if it did happen again.

Without knowing where they would be staying while they were in Florida, Sage ordered a taxi, leaving his bike at the bar since they had both been drinking, and decided that he and Mia would stay at a hotel for the night until they made living arrangements the next day. He made sure that this time they would get separate rooms. He couldn't risk anything else happening that night. He had already crossed the line.

But he couldn't stop himself from playing it over and over again in his head when he got in his room. The way her body had felt and reacted to his touch had been a thrill for him. She just wanted to please him and he loved that. He couldn't stop thinking about her soft lips, and how smooth her skin felt beneath his hands. He went to bed that night thinking of their bodies connecting over and over again.

---

$\mathcal{M}$ia could tell that Sage had almost immediately drawn back from her after their moment in the back office. Once they had left the office, Sage went to the bar for another drink and proceeded to act as though nothing had happened. She did not regret it happening though as she had been waiting for it for so long but she had to put that aside because she had no idea where Sage and herself would be staying in Florida. They could not live out of a hotel during their stay as who knew how long they'd be in Florida for.

She decided to take a walk to a cafe close to the hotel so she could connect her phone to the internet and start searching for houses in the area. She would look into a two-bedroom place, nothing too pricey although she began to wonder just how they would pay for a place considering neither of them had much to their names.

It was in the morning just after she had bookmarked a few houses when she received a text message from her banking account that showed a rather large lump sum had been deposited into her account. Shocked, Mia looked into the details of the transfer; it had come from Fiona. Mia decided to give Fiona a call to double-check that there hadn't been a mix-up. She had never had that much money in her account before and she honestly didn't know how to respond to it.

It was on the third ring that Fiona picked up.

"Hello?" Fiona asked through the phone.

"Hi, Fiona, it's Mia," she said.

"Oh, Mia, hello. I really should save your number into my phone but I keep getting distracted," Fiona said with a slight laugh.

"Haha, I'm sure you'll get around to it," Mia said.

"I will indeed. Well, I'm assuming there is a reason you called. Has something happened?" she asked.

"Oh no, nothing has happened. I just wanted to verify an amount that got transferred to my account. It's a rather huge amount of money and I just wanted to make sure there hasn't been a mix up somewhere," Mia said.

"You didn't expect me to send you and Sage to Florida without sorting you both out, did you? You'll need money to live off of and it just so happens that the Screaming Demons has recently come into a lot of it thanks to the Omens," Fiona said.

"Oh, so the money is for myself and Sage to live off?" Mia asked, just wanting to make sure she had gotten the information correct.

"Yes, yes, that's right," she replied, saying as if she were waving her hands around to dismiss the stupid topic. Mia was truly grateful to Fiona for taking care of both her and Sage. She hadn't had the slightest clue what they would've done without the help.

" Thank you so much, Fiona. It's really appreciated," she said.

"Well, you're welcome. Now I've also sorted out a house for the both of you. I need you both to live there, for safety reasons," Fiona said.

Mia could already tell that it would be awkward between herself and Sage as he had already started to ignore her. Was the sex bad for him then, she wondered.

"Oh, Fiona, that's so wonderful. Thank you so much again. I will definitely tell Sage the good news. I'm sure he'll be pleased," Mia said, even though she knew that was a lie.

"Look, Mia, all I need you to worry about is the club. Now I have to go and sort out some business. Please keep me updated with regards to what happens," she said.

"Yes, of course, Fiona." And with that, the phone went dead.

It was within a few minutes that she got a text message with the address of her new home, a home she would have to share with Sage. She knew that it would be hard but they didn't have a choice. Fiona sounded extremely serious about them living together and Mia would do anything to make sure Fiona knew she was listening and doing as she was told so she could earn her trust back. Even if that meant living with someone who clearly wanted to be as far away from her as possible.

Mia couldn't help but feel a little hurt by Sage's attitude toward her. When they had gotten to the hotel the previous night, Sage had been adamant at reception that they needed separate rooms and for the first time on the entire trip he didn't join Mia for dinner, and she couldn't imagine why. Sage wanted her just as much as she wanted him and she knew that so why was he acting this way toward her, she wondered. If he regretted it then Mia supposed there wouldn't be much she could do but he didn't have to snub her. She was a big girl and he could just be honest with her. She wouldn't fight it.

Mia tried to push it out of her mind as she had other things to take care of. First, she had to go collect the keys. Fiona had left them with the relator so Mia took it upon herself to call a taxi and head out. Sage had already left his room. She found that out when she reached reception and she was informed that both rooms had already been taken care of. He was definitely avoiding her. He had never just left her before even the night after they had gotten carried away in the hotel room but she supposed that was only because he had to bring her here. Maybe he would've left her there if he could've.

Mia looked at her phone and hesitated for a few seconds before she dialed his number so she could inform him about the living arrangements. She'd have to tell him somehow, even though she already knew he wouldn't be happy about it. He picked up on the first ring.

"Hello, Mia." Clearly, he had her number saved, unlike Fiona. He sounded so formal over the phone, it was beginning to feel as though the night before had never actually happened. She knew it had, she could still feel his lips on her skin, she could still remember him kissing her freckles across her shoulders; she hadn't made that up.

"Hey, Sage, um, I'm just calling to let you know about the living situation. Fiona told me this morning that there's a house already waiting for us. I'm heading out now to pick up the keys," Mia said. She had had a dream about them being together not that long ago. She had pictured them living together but she never imagined it would be like this.

"I was meaning to come by your room to tell you that

I had headed to the bar to pick up my bike but I didn't want to disturb you." She could tell that was a lie. She knew he just didn't want to see her. The sting of rejection got a whole lot worse. Why couldn't he just be honest with her?

"Oh don't worry about that," she said as she tried to act like it didn't matter. "I'll send you a message with the details of the house so you know where to go."

"Thanks, Mia, I'll see you later then," Sage said just before he hung up.

Mia couldn't let herself think of Sage too much. If she did, it would just hurt, so she had to distract herself and although she knew the money was for living expenses, she decided that it would be a good idea to get a few art supplies. After all, she did want to focus some of her time on art again.

After collecting the keys she asked the taxi driver to take her to the best art supply store in town.

She wasn't disappointed when she walked into the store. It was covered in row after row of paints, acrylics, paintbrushes, canvases in all sizes. She could not contain her excitement as she walked through every aisle picking out all the things she'd need to start from scratch. She knew she shouldn't go overboard so she only bought the things she knew she would need to start at a beginner's level.

After she had done her shopping she headed to the

house. Upon arrival, she was completely taken aback by how huge the house was. From the outside, she thought it must have at least six bedrooms, for what Mia didn't understand. She thought it looked like one of those houses that you see on TV, where famous people show you how extravagantly they live. Fiona had seriously outdone herself. Mia had never lived in a house that had more than two rooms. When she had been struggling just off the streets, she lived in a studio apartment where nothing was separated. You'd go from the kitchen straight into the lounge which would be turned into a bedroom late at night with a tiny bathroom on the side. She couldn't imagine how it would feel now living in a house almost the size of a mansion.

She entered the house and took the time to walk around every inch of it. She had to take it all in to even believe 100 percent that she was actually there and that the house was actually real. It all felt like a dream to her. She knew she still had a lot to prove and to make right with Grier and Fiona but they were seriously the nicest people she had met. Who on earth would give anyone a house like this along with a rather large lump sum of money?

She had been close, there were seven rooms. Four bedrooms, two looked like main bedrooms with larger beds than the other two rooms. All rooms were decorated with grey bedding, fluffy white rugs, with matching headboards and bedside table set. The beds all looked extremely comfortable and if she were a child she would definitely have jumped on all of the beds in turn. There were three offices and she already knew she'd claim one for herself. They all had a large mahogany desk and a leather-backed chair, and all the desks had computers already installed in place. She noted a huge kitchen, extremely elegant looking with mostly white walls and clean marble lining the countertops, and all the cupboards were already packed with all the utensils they'd need for cooking as well as a fully stocked fridge. There were six toilets, four being ensuites and the others for guests. There were four garages although Mia didn't have a car and Sage only had his bike.

The interior of the house was extremely warm and inviting, mostly lush browns and soft pillows scattered across the couches that occupied the two lounges the house had. There was one dining area. The house was something Mia had never dreamed of living in and she was extremely grateful to get the opportunity.

Sage only arrived at the house in the evening, once Mia had already made dinner and settled into the house. He took a tour of the house by myself and without saying a word to Mia, he chose one of the rooms at the far end of the house. Mia definitely knew that he was ignoring her. Although she had been pretty confident about it before, this just confirmed it for her.

Well, Sage had made it clear that he didn't need Mia around that much. She decided to make one of the offices into her art room and constantly distracted herself with painting whenever she got emotional over the situation. She couldn't stand how she had begun to feel, again feeling like she didn't belong. She couldn't let her emotions get the best of her though, she still had to maintain some sort of composure.

Over the next couple of days, Mia had barely seen Sage. He would constantly leave her at the house while he would go to the bar. They had been sent together to run the bar but Sage had begun to make it extremely uncomfortable. Why does he have to act this way, Mia thought.

One night Mia could no longer take him ignoring her and she decided to go look for him throughout the housing, finding him in the farthest room in the house.

## 12

Sage had spent the last few days trying to ignore Mia, it was easy enough when he had the bar to go to and so he would often leave her at the house to get away. She had been nice to him, constantly making sure he had food to eat, and she never brought up the way he had started to treat her. He knew that it wasn't the ideal situation and he also knew that she couldn't be happy with it but to Sage, there was nothing else he could do. He needed to separate himself even if that meant hurting her feelings which he knew he did. It was just something he thought would be for better for them both. They were there for business, that was it. He was extremely irritated with Fiona for putting him in this position so he had to call her to let her know how he felt about it.

She picked up almost immediately.

"Hello, Sage," she said. "How are you finding Florida?" she asked.

"Fiona, Florida would be better if you hadn't forced me to live with Mia," he stated, cutting to the chase. How could she do this, he thought. She was just asking for trouble. Had someone told her about what happened at the bar? Did she think it would be fun to torture them even more by making them live together? No, everyone had been distracted by women giving them lap dances, no one had even noticed their absence, Sage thought.

"Oh, Sage, what's the big deal? I've put you two together in a huge house. Why are you making this into an issue?" Fiona asked. She was playing dumb and Sage knew it. She had known exactly what putting them together would do, right at the beginning, she had known.

"You know why it's an issue," he said.

"If you feel like the physical attraction you both have for each other will be a problem then stay in one of the rooms at the far end of the house," she said matter of factly.

"Well, that's exactly what I'll have to do, isn't it?" he said.

"See? Problem solved. You'll live in the house with Mia just as I want you to and you'll stay at the opposite side of the house," Fiona said.

"Okay, fine. I guess that will have to do," he said as his initial anger started to fade.

"Good boy, now I have to go. Make sure everything runs smoothly there, Sage. I'm counting on both of you," Fiona said just as she hung up.

Sage knew that Mia wasn't right for him. He found her attractive that was for sure but like he had sensed from the very beginning, she was just bad news. She seemed to have always been bad news, and because of that she just attracted it into her life. She had constantly been mixed up with the wrong people. First the drug dealers she used to work for, then being an addict herself, she didn't value her life like Sage did. He had come close to death so many times and he had always been grateful to have survived but he had never been reckless with his life. He had always put his life on the line for the greater good, but he definitely could not say the same for Mia. She just didn't seem to have a huge regard for human life. She had gotten herself mixed up with the Omens which is technically the only reason Sage was stuck with her, otherwise, he would only have been bumping into her at the bar like he usually did. He probably never would have had sex with her either. She was a feisty person but she was too quick to act, too naive, and lacked the maturity he needed from a woman. One minute she would be all over him and the next she would be irritated with every little thing he did.

She blew hot and cold way too much for his liking. Sage needed a woman he could always rely on. He would never have to question her loyalty nor would he have to question what she would do next because she would be so constant with her actions. Mia was not that person for him.

The next thing Sage knew, Mia was there in his room, distracting him from his train of thought. She looked so sexy, he thought. She let herself in, looking around the room as she entered.

"So I guess you've chosen your room then," she said as she noticed his clothes had been brought out of his bag. It would also seem as though he had bought some more since there were a lot more clothes than what they had brought with them.

"Yes, I think this is for the best," he said. He couldn't look her in the eyes.

She was in her almost see-through pajamas again and Sage could see her nipples peeking through.

Don't look, he thought, she must've done this on purpose.

"Why is it for the best, Sage?" she asked as she sat on the bed next to him. She positioned herself so her body was pointing directly at him, deliberately making him unable to look anywhere else but at her when he turned to his side to face her.

"We're here for business, Mia. What happened the

other night can't happen again," he said. Although he wanted it to happen so badly.

"Did you not enjoy it?" she asked. Sage could tell the thought of that hurt her. He could see it written on her face.

"Mia, how could you think I didn't enjoy it…? It was amazing. I was left speechless," he said. He had to be honest with her which seemed to help lift her mood again.

"So then surely it can't be that bad, then? Surely it could happen again?" she said with hope in her voice. They both wanted each other and Sage knew that. But he had to resist, although he couldn't help himself from looking at her nipples every now and again, wishing he could cup her breasts in his hands.

Mia moved forward, shifting herself closer to him. She was getting too close and yet Sage could not bring himself to move away. He was captivated by her. Her eyes hadn't left his and he could see the desire burning in them. Just by looking at her, his body was overcome by a sense of need and longing.

She reached over and placed one hand on his thigh, slowly running it up and down, teasing him. He couldn't move. She leaned across and proceeded to kiss his neck. It was too late, he couldn't stop her now.

He reached for her greedily, wanting his hands all over her body. She didn't fight it; she moaned at his touch which just turned him on even further. He found her lips and soon their mouths and tongues were all over each other. He wasted no time and pulled her top off, kissing and gently sucking at her breasts and nipples which were hard to the touch. Mia reached her hand across and felt his erection through his jeans. She wanted all of him and she wanted him now. Soon they had tugged and pulled at each other's clothes, almost ripping them off in a frenzy of bodies and hands reaching and touching at exposed skin. Neither of them having the patience to take it slowly. They both were desperate for each other.

Sage gently pushed Mia back so she was lying on her back across the bed. He took a moment to take all of her in. She was mesmerizing, lying fully naked on his bed. He leaned down, kissing and licking at her skin. He could tell she was ready and lord knew he was ready too, so he reached for a condom from his cupboard, opened it and positioned himself over her. Soon their bodies connected and all that echoed throughout the house was the sound of them losing themselves in each other. Their hands never left the other's body, fingers gripping onto skin, locking each other as they moved their bodies in time, finding a pattern, connecting in a way they hadn't the first time.

The first time had been amazing. It had been dirty and hot, filled with exploring new skin, but this time had been different. The second time was filled with desire and need, needing each other to be close, needing the contact of the other person's body on theirs. Sage knew they had crossed the line again but this time he couldn't think of much else other than Mia's naked body under his. They soon both let go, finally giving in to the sensations their bodies were feeling.

They lay on the bed, having never gotten under the covers in their rush, and continued to breathe heavily as they both tried to catch their breaths. The room felt 100 degrees hotter as both of them were slightly covered in sweat. They didn't move, they didn't talk, they just lay there coming back to reality.

Sage knew that this would change everything. They hadn't just done it once now but twice and he couldn't help but wonder if it would just continue to happen even when he tried to fight it. Mia had a way with him. She could do one thing that would just overrun his logical thinking and even though it was exciting and she was definitely something worth getting excited over he was unsure of whether it would help if they continued the way they were. However, he could not deny that he would continue to want her.

Mia soon fell asleep, right in Sage's bed. Her body was spent and she didn't think she was capable of moving back to her room. Sage didn't move her nor did he move himself. Sleeping next to Mia hadn't happened much and he felt like he just wanted to feel her body next to his in case they both got the strength to stay away from each other from here on out. He pulled her sleeping body into his and wrapped his arms around her. She nuzzled her head into his chest and took a deep breath in. Although she was sleeping she felt completely at ease. Sage soon found himself drifting off into a deep sleep, where Mia was the only thing he could see. Her brown, honey-like eyes, her dark short hair and her pixie-like ears filled his mind along with freckles, freckles everywhere.

## 13

$S$age usually dreamt of being in Afghanistan when he went to bed. The attack that had happened to him and his team played out behind his closed eyelids, always ending in the same way. He could never escape it, his past constantly taunting him in his sleep. It had been a traumatic experience that his mind would constantly go back to when he was unconscious and he, unfortunately, had no control over it. He didn't know why he couldn't move on past it after all the time that had passed by but he thought it could have something to do with the guilt he felt. He had tried sleeping pills in the hopes that they would just knock him out cold, but he could never escape the dream, even then. Sometimes he was lucky, and he wouldn't dream at all. Those nights he loved because it was always so much easier than reliving his own personal hell. He could imagine hell being that moment played over and over for him to relive constantly.

*He would usually be helpless in the dream, standing stuck in one place watching as the bombs went off, never touching him but always ripping through his team. The sense was always exactly like the real one. No walls to hide behind and bullets flying everywhere. He felt like he was constantly covered by an invisible shield that could not be penetrated, and all he wanted to do was help them. He had watched them die night after night in his sleep while he stood as a spectator. Sometimes in his dreams, his teammates would yell at him for help but every time he tried to move, nothing would happen. His arms remained at his sides and even though it felt like he was using every single muscle he had in his body to reach out to help, he could never reach them. He'd watch as Laura would call out to him, reaching for him with her bloody fingers. He'd cry out to her, he could feel his mouth moving, but words would never come out.*

*"I'm so sorry!" he yelled at her and the rest of his team.*

*"How could you leave us here?!" he could hear them yell at him.*

*"I couldn't help it," he'd cry out. "I'm trying, I really am!"*

*"You should be with us!" they'd all cry out at the same time.*

In his dream, he would agree with them, but still, nothing would change. He'd watch his teammates die once again. Sometimes he'd wake up before anything too graphic happened, but other times he'd still be there after the dust had settled from the bomb and all he could see were body parts scattered around him. He would scream in his sleep, sometimes it would wake him up.

He thought he would never know what a proper peaceful night of sleep would be like ever again.

He carried the guilt of being the only survivor with him every day, and when he woke up from his dreams, he'd be covered in sweat, with his heartbeat racing in his ears. He had constantly woken up feeling tired while his muscles would scream at him. He knew he had probably been tensing his body throughout his dream, probably also thrashing around in his bed throughout the night. There weren't many nights where he had a peaceful night's sleep. He had begun to think he would never sleep peacefully again. He had thought about going to see someone about his sleeping problems, but he felt it wouldn't help. Unless they could remove his memory, he would be stuck just the way he was.

When he woke up the next morning unable to remember having had a dream, he was a little stunned. He hadn't slept so well in so long that when he lay next to Mia, he tried to cherish the one peaceful night's sleep he had had while she was by his side. His body didn't feel sore, and he wasn't covered in his own sweat, which was extremely pleasant. He didn't want to sound insane and say it was thanks to her that he had managed to make it through the night without having a horrible dream, but a part of him knew that it must have had something to do with her being there. He felt so at ease when he was around her, and clearly, her charm worked on him even when he was sleeping. Although it was nice to wake up from a peaceful night's sleep, he couldn't sleep with Mia every night just to avoid his bad dreams. It didn't work that way, and unfortunately, he knew it couldn't happen again.

He had woken up before her and decided it would be better for him not to be in bed with her when she woke up. He had spent the night with her, and already that was crossing the line. He knew he should have slept somewhere else. The house had other rooms he could've slept in even if it had been the couch in the lounge, but Mia's soft skin against his had been almost impossible for him to leave and so he had ended up staying. He ran one finger slowly down her one exposed arm as he just wanted one last touch before he would have to leave her. She sighed in her sleep, and her eyes flickered a bit, but she didn't wake. She appeared to be a heavy sleeper. Sage tried to compare something to how smooth her skin was but nothing came to his mind. He wished he could stay there with her but he knew he couldn't.

He got out of bed and had one final look at Mia, he took a mental picture of just how beautiful she looked while she slept, it seemed that she was beautiful no matter what she was doing. She lay naked under the covers with just her arms showing as they were cradling her face on top of her pillow. The sun was shining through the curtains so she was slightly lit up. To Sage, it looked like she was glowing, especially her hair that didn't look as black in the sunlight but a very dark brown. Her lips were slightly parted as she breathed deeply in and out, still hypnotized by whatever dream she was having. It was hard for Sage to see her like that, vulnerable and unaware of the effect she had on him, he was finding it hard to keep himself detached, but he knew that he had to. He hadn't loved anyone since Laura, and he doubted he ever would. She had been the love of his life, and he never wanted to feel like he was letting her go by letting someone else in. Sage knew that that was one of the reasons why he wouldn't let Mia in.

It wasn't just about work like he tried to convince himself it was, but it was more about the fact that he would never get the future he had planned and he didn't want to just replace the girl in his future. He felt like letting Mia in would mean he was replacing Laura. He knew they were two very different people who were nothing like each other, but it felt like he could never have a future with anyone because Laura hadn't gotten a chance to have her own future and a future with him.

The sex was amazing, and he couldn't deny that

whenever she was around him and touching him, he was completely intoxicated by her like nothing he had ever experienced before. She had a pull about her that his body was just drawn to, like a moth to a flame. He knew it would only end badly and as much as he enjoyed it he would do anything to make sure he didn't allow his feelings to get involved because he could not end up getting attached to another person who may leave him. He had to keep reminding himself of that. It's just a fling, he told himself, hoping that would make him feel better about the situation. It didn't. As hard as he tried, he knew Mia could be good for him. He had seen it so many times since they had met. She was stronger than anyone he had been with but he still didn't want to risk it. His emotions in the past had only brought him pain and he could not do that to himself once again, not willingly at least because he knew the outcome.

He knew it would be better for both of them for it all to stop. They were both there for business and it would only end in disaster if anything went wrong between them like most things had in his life. He wasn't sure if he could risk it. He had a duty to the Screaming Demons, a duty to Fiona and he could only imagine it ending badly for all parties if things went sour between the two of them. He had searched for a purpose for so long after the army that he would not risk what he had made for himself within the Screaming Demons. He knew they respected him because he didn't try to make himself out to be bigger and better than them. He rather tried to get to know them as friends so he knew they'd always be comfortable around him, even in difficult situations.

He headed to the bathroom so he could shower and clear his mind. He turned on the water and waited for steam to fill the bathroom before he stepped into the shower. He had always enjoyed making an almost sauna effect while showering and he loved to shower in extremely hot water to get rid of the sweat he was usually covered in. As he proceeded to wash his hair and wash his body he convinced himself that he was also washing the last bits of Mia away, off of his skin and hopefully out of his mind but he couldn't help but replay the night before. He could almost feel Mia around him. He closed his eyes and sighed picturing Mia naked. His body reacted to the images almost instantly. He knew he should not be thinking about her like that, especially if he was going to try to stop things between them but the image of her laying in his bed only a few feet away wouldn't stop running through his mind.

What he'd do to be next to her, kissing her, touching her and inside her... You need to forget it, he told himself. Mia was sexy, and he found her extremely attractive, which definitely did not help his case. He knew that being so close to Mia on a daily basis would definitely become a problem, but he also knew that he could not get out of the house due to Fiona's strict instructions and so he would have to try and stay busy in an attempt to keep himself away from her. He finished in the shower and then got dressed as quickly and as quietly as he could to not disturb Mia. Luckily she had stayed fast asleep.

He made himself a coffee and sat quietly in the lounge. He had never bothered himself with the task of making breakfast in the mornings. He could survive until midday without eating. He had learned in the army how to preserve himself for long periods of time. It hadn't been days of course, but he could hold out on food for a good few hours. He usually had a big lunch and a big dinner to make up for his lack of breakfast. He couldn't say he was a good cook, so he didn't end up cooking much, but he tried ordering healthy meals whenever he could. He knew it was important to get the right amount of nutrients into his body. He had to maintain a healthy lifestyle so he could maintain his physical strength. He was fortunate enough to have been born with a pretty strong body without much training, but he loved the adrenaline he would get from a good work out. He continued to sip his coffee, and just as he was about to head out, he quickly placed the mug in the sink.

He noticed that Mia had started cleaning around the house and as much as he tried, he would always be in too much of a rush to bother cleaning up after himself. He tried to remain tidy and neat in his room, but he sometimes left dirty dishes lying around. He had grown up in a family where his mother was a stay at home mom who would clean up around everyone. He felt a little guilty about it, but he wasn't used to having to clean up after himself even though he was a grown man.

He left the house and decided to distract himself with work. After all, that was what he had been sent there to do, not fuck Mia, even if it had felt great at the time, better than great he had to admit. He tried to focus on work, looking after the club, and making sure everything was running smoothly. He had started to monitor the Omens that were in town but hadn't found any suspicious behavior, so it seemed everything was under control. He would exchange emails and calls with Grier that had to do with the chop shops and some of the other work he had started doing on the side. He knew it was dangerous, but he knew what he was doing, so he was never worried about getting caught. He had trained to be a sniper when he had been in the army. Although he never went down that road, he still knew how to be sneaky if nothing else. Grier had trusted him with the projects, and Sage knew he would stop at nothing until it was done.

Day in and day out, Sage tried to continue with his previous plan, keeping his distance from Mia. He had tried and failed in the beginning, but he knew this time he had to make it work. He had begun to constantly leave for work before she would wake up and he'd get home as late as possible so she would already be asleep. The house may be big, but there was no way to avoid her if he didn't try. He was lucky that he worked for Grier and she worked for Fiona. That way he knew he was unlikely to bump into her during the day while he was out and about doing jobs and such for Grier. He couldn't deny that he had started to miss seeing her every day but he still had a strong sense that he was doing the right thing. After all, she seemed to have gotten the sense that something was up because she hadn't done anything to confront him about the situation. Maybe she also knew it was for the best, but he didn't know. He would sometimes smell her perfume through the house as he returned home, which made it extremely hard because in those moments he wouldn't have minded just curling up next to her in bed while she slept.

It had been working so far as Sage had managed not to bump into Mia in a few days but it had begun to take a toll on him and so he decided to stop for a drink at the bar on his way home. He was completely taken aback when he walked through the doors and saw Mia standing and laughing with the new Hell Kats near the entrance of the club.

He did not know what to do because he had not expected to see her there. He knew she wasn't a big drinker because that was something they had in common, but he could tell she had been having a good time, she had a smile across her face just before she saw him and only then did it change into a blank stare. Clearly, he wasn't the only one who was a little shocked. He had no other choice but to just ignore her. In his mind it was the only thing he could do that would stop anything from happening and so as he walked right into the bar and continued to walk straight past her, making a beeline for the bar without looking in her direction. He tried to keep his eyes on the ground so as not to risk looking at her. He had already gotten a glimpse of her when he walked in, and that was almost enough to unravel him. He had definitely missed her smile and the dimples that formed on the sides of her cheeks. Stop it, Sage, he yelled at himself internally, he couldn't break now.

Shit, he thought. He had gone to the bar to get away from her, and yet there she was, looking as beautiful and as distracting as ever. Just ignore her, he told himself, don't let her presence get to you. He could tell she was following him with her eyes as he walked past her toward the bar. He could feel them boring into his back as he took a seat at the bar. Sage made the mistake of turning around to look at her face and immediately regretted it. Her face just screamed hurt and pain, and he hated that he had caused it, but he had to do what was best for both of them, and he felt that it was best that nothing would go anything further. He knew it hurt her, it would hurt anyone, but if she understood it from his point of view, she would see that he was just trying to stop her from getting hurt further down the line. Unfortunately, she couldn't read his mind and Sage knew she would hate him going forward. He thought that having her hate him would make everything a lot easier because then at least she would stop trying to pursue him and it would give her a reason to look for someone better than Sage. He just wasn't ready to be emotionally involved with anyone yet and unfortunately, he didn't think he'd be able to admit that to anyone.

He did not want to hurt her on purpose, and he knew if he had just kept his distance in the first place he wouldn't have to act like he didn't care about her when he actually did care about her. He probably cared about her more than she thought but he knew that it would work out better for both of them if he didn't lead her on. He hoped she wouldn't stay long, he really didn't want to leave just yet because the bar was a good way to distract himself. He had never been a bad guy, he had never mistreated a woman, and so he could sense that Mia was going to be the first person who felt that way about him. He hated that he was now making a bad reputation for himself.

He watched in the mirror that ran along the bar as she stood at the door for a few seconds. She had turned to look at him once again, and he could see her reflection clear as day in the mirror. She still had a look of shock and hurt written all over her face. She had gotten the message though because she didn't try to talk to him and she clearly didn't want to stay because she then turned and said her goodbyes to the Hell Kats and left. Sage felt bad, but he was also relieved. If she had come up to him and tried to talk to him he would have had to be dramatic, and he didn't want to cause a scene in the bar in front of everyone. He knew no one would get involved if he had, but he did not want to embarrass Mia in front of so many people, especially considering they were supposed to be working with each other and not against each other.

As Sage sat at the bar, the rest of the Screaming Demons there welcomed him. Some people had noticed the exchange between himself and Mia, but no one dared to say anything. Soon a whiskey neat was placed in front of him. He was already respected, and each bartender knew what he drank.

"Thanks, man," he said to the bartender. Needing a sip as quickly as possible to calm his nerves after seeing Mia standing there just minutes ago.

"No problem, sir. Needing a quick drink before you head home for tonight?" the bartender asked.

He was a friendly enough bartender, but Sage was in no mood to talk. However, he didn't want to be rude. He was never rude unless really necessary, and right then he had no reason to be rude to the bartender.

"Yeah, it's been a rather busy week," Sage replied, keeping it short and sweet.

"Business-wise or pleasure?" the bartender winked at him.

It hadn't taken long before the footage of Mia and Sage in the office had gotten out. Luckily people had a lot of respect for him outside of work, so no one really dared mention it, but it was definitely known around the Screaming Demons in Florida.

"Excuse me, what did you say?" Sage asked. He could not believe what he had heard. Everyone knew their place and knew that if they mentioned anything, it could only lead to trouble. Sage stared the bartender down. Looking at him, Sage could tell he was trying to push some buttons. Clearly, it had been a slow day for him, and he now felt the need to make some entertainment for himself.

"Oh well, you know, you don't always have to be busy just doing work," the bartender said. He looked at Sage with a deadpan stare. Clearly, because the bartender had seen Mia there too, he must have thought something else would go down again. Sage decided it wasn't worth his time, so he decided to let it go.

"I guess business is the only thing on my mind," Sage said matter of factly. He did not want to give the guy another chance to take the conversation any further. The bartender got the message though and turned away, moving along to serve other customers at the bar.

Sage continued to sip his whiskey, trying to bide his time before heading home.

After he had finished his first drink, he decided to order another whiskey neat along with a glass of water. He didn't want to get drunk, but he knew he'd have to wait a little while longer before leaving. Mia hadn't left too long ago so there was no chance she'd be asleep yet.

He sat at the bar and let his mind zone in on the music that was playing in the background. He no longer wanted to think about Mia, but just as he had started to get into a good zone, slowly bobbing his head to the music, he heard yelling and screaming coming from outside the bar and just as he was about to head out to see what was going on, a man entered the bar.

Sage could instantly tell he meant trouble because he was wearing the Omens' colors. The man continued to yell as he walked in, and it took Sage a while to fully understand what he was saying until it all clicked.

"You're all murderers!" the man yelled. "You call yourselves the Screaming Demons, but you should call yourselves the Murdering Demons!" he continued to shout. It was obvious to Sage that the man was referring to the killing of Tyler, but he couldn't have been this dumb to walk into the Screaming Demons bar and expect a warm welcome. Everyone around town knew what had happened with Tyler back home and Sage found it completely unbelievable that this man who was clearly an Omen would just walk into a bar full of his enemies.

Sage and a few other men around the bar got up and started to make their way over to the man, allowing Sage to lead the way while the rest of the men all trailed behind him. They were all ready for a fight.

"Come on, man, I don't think you know what you're doing. Maybe it would be best if you just leave now before this goes any further," Sage said. He wasn't in the mood to fight, but if it turned into that, he knew that he would have to defend the Screaming Demons. It was his duty.

"I know exactly what I'm doing!" he started to shout. "You think you're all so tough, but you're all killers! You'll pay for what you've done to Tyler!" the man yelled. He hadn't moved further into the bar considering Sage was standing before him with at least six men on his heels all ready to attack whenever Sage gave the order. He pointed his finger at every person in the bar indicating that his threat was for everyone. The man clearly hadn't gotten the picture that the Screaming Demons were not to be messed with.

All the frustration that had been building up in Sage over the past few days had reached a breaking point, and this guy was just pushing him even further. He zeroed in on him, allowing himself to let go of some of the pent up frustration.

First, he pushed the guy, trying to edge him out of the bar, but he was standing firm, so Sage then swung his arm around and knocked the guy straight to the floor. He felt a surge of power and adrenaline course through his veins. It felt good to release. He did not fully understand just how much frustration had been building up. The situation with Mia was affecting him more than he had thought.

"I. Told. You. To. Get. Out," he said between each kick. He laid into the guy who had put himself into the fetal position on the floor. After a few kicks, Sage stopped. He needed to send a message to the Omens. "Now, get the fuck out of here and send a message to the rest of the Omens. The Screaming Demons now run this town and we will get rid of anyone who gets in our way."

Sage walked back to the bar to down the remains of his drink while the men picked the guy up and kicked him out of the bar. Everyone in the bar had kept silent while everything had been happening, and just as the

Screaming Demons reentered the bar, everyone erupted into a cheer.

The bartender walked over with a fresh drink. "This one's on the house, sir," he said. It was clear that from watching what Sage was capable of, the bartender knew not to ever cross the line again.

"Thanks," Sage said as he brought the fresh drink to his lips. Although he had every intention of leaving after his second drink, he needed a bit more time to get his adrenaline and heart rate back to normal before he left so he decided to wait at least another hour before he headed out.

---

$\mathcal{M}$ia had woken up alone the day after she had had sex with Sage. It had been amazing. She knew she had started it, but he definitely finished it. He had left without saying goodbye. She woke up feeling like a completely new person. Her body felt good in every way possible and she knew it was thanks to Sage. He made her feel so many things, passion, ecstasy, want, need and all things that could be linked to being completely satisfied. She was surprised when she could feel her body craving more just as she woke up. She could spend the whole day and night with Sage and still it wouldn't be enough. She stretched out, pointing her toes as her legs went stiff, into a really good morning stretch. She then stretched her arms out to feel the space he should've been in, but her hands were empty. She opened her eyes and saw that the bed was empty, no Sage in sight. She sat up straight in the bed and sat in silence for a while, wondering if she'd be able to hear him somewhere else in the house, but she couldn't. He clearly wasn't in the house anymore, and she didn't think too much of it at the time. She got dressed back into her clothes from the night before because even if she was alone she didn't want to walk around the house naked and she wasn't willing to take any of Sage's clothes just in case that upset him. She then walked past his bathroom and found he had showered. Steam was still hanging in the air along with the smell of body wash, cologne, and toothpaste. She walked back to her room. He had obviously left for work, and maybe he didn't want to wake me, she thought.

She felt extremely exhausted all of a sudden and decided that she'd just go back to sleep in her own bed. She didn't have any work to do that day so no one would miss her if she took a day to herself and so she climbed back into her bed and within seconds she was fast asleep yet again.

She woke up a few hours later feeling extremely happy with the outcome of the night before. She honestly didn't think it would be that easy since Sage had been trying to distance himself from her, but he soon gave in to her, and they had melted into each other. Mia lay in her bed with the memory of his lips on hers, then on her skin. The thought of it sent a shiver through her body. She couldn't deny that she wanted him more than ever. She had never had her body touched the way he had touched her. It was a feeling of passion as well as complete awe, as if her body was amazing to him like she was a piece of art beneath his fingertips. She felt treasured under his touch, she felt amazing. Her body responded to him so easily when he was near as if she could tell his next move so she could match her body to his. It was powerful and overwhelming, and she obviously enjoyed it. She had never really had bad sex with anyone else, but there was something about the way their bodies moved together that just made it more pleasurable.

It was almost as if their bodies were somehow connected to each other, and she could feel deep down that it was possible that they shared a connection neither of them could deny.

Once she had laid in bed for long enough, reliving the memory of Sage and the night before, she decided it was time for her to at least do something with what was left of her day.

She got up and took a shower. She needed to cleanse herself after sleeping for so long. She didn't even want to think of all the dead skin cells she had all over her body. Mia was someone who believed in showering twice a day, once in the morning to get everything off of her skin from the night before and then once before she went to bed so she could rinse off the day she had been through. Even if she hadn't been that busy that day, she knew there were constant germs flying around in the air and she didn't want them on her while she slept because that was her most vulnerable state and it would be so easy for an infection of some sort to attack her body. As she proceeded to step into the shower, she washed her hair. She loved the smell of her shampoo because it smelt like strawberries and lavender, her two favorite scents. Once she had washed her hair thoroughly, she washed her face and the rest of her body. She stepped out of the shower completely clean and feeling refreshed and continued to smother her skin with lotion and blow-dry her hair. She put a pair of fresh jeans on with a shirt that was just comfortable enough to lounge around the house in but not smart or casual enough to go anywhere in.

Since Sage had left for work and she didn't have much to do, she went and got his laundry from his room and did his washing and then her own. She lounged around the house a bit while she waited and found a movie on tv to watch while she waited. After about an hour she heard the ping go off from the washing machine, and so she unloaded the washing machine and proceeded to hang all the clean clothes on the line outside in the garden. She would've just set the machine to tumble dry but she had always had a bad experience with tumble drying her clothes. Something would always shrink when it wasn't supposed to, or something ended up lost; who knew where it went.

It was actually a beautiful day considering she had woken up so late and so she decided to take herself outside so she could soak up some vitamin D. She hadn't been much of a swimmer when she was growing up and even went she got older she preferred staying on dry land so she didn't bother going into the pool. Instead, she put some music on the surround sound and just sat in the sun for a while. Enjoying the day, she couldn't complain because she felt so happy at that moment. She thought that there could be a chance for her and Sage to develop into something and with the beautiful sky above her, she left like anything was possible, and she believed it.

She closed her eyes as she continued to lay in the sun. She listened to the birds chirping in the trees above her, and she felt at peace. After a while, she headed back inside. She didn't want to risk getting sunburnt, and she was getting rather hungry.

She headed for the kitchen and made herself a toasted cheese sandwich, it had been a while since she last had one and they reminded her of happy days while growing up, so it seemed fitting for her current mood.

Mia then collected the clothes off of the line so she could press them and place them back in their places. It doesn't take her long to do both her clothes and Sage's clothes, but she took the time to make sure everything was folded neatly so it wouldn't cause any unnecessary creasing. She headed to Sage's room so she could place all of his clothes back where they belonged. Then she made his bed because she always preferred to have a neat and tidy bed to come home to. She then cleaned up his bathroom as some of his products were just lying around the sink. After she was satisfied with his room, she closed the door out of respect and headed back to the kitchen. She had forgotten to clean up after herself.

She cleaned the kitchen and cleaned her room after she had placed her own clothes back. It was still early enough for her to rest before she made dinner. She had had a rather busy and domesticated morning, and she felt that she deserved a break, so she took a seat back on the couch in the lounge and found another movie to watch.

Once the movie had finished, she made some dinner, leaving some extra food for Sage considering he hadn't made it home for dinner. She sat at the dining room table by herself and ate alone. She wasn't sure what time Sage would be home from work, so she decided to head off to bed. Although she hadn't done any work regarding the business and the Hell Kats, she was definitely exhausted. She climbed into bed, resting her head on her pillow, and she soon fell asleep with Sage on her mind.

* * *

SHE WASN'T sure if Sage was ignoring her or if he had just left without wanting to disturb her, but he remained out late that night and again left the following morning before she could see him. She was slowly beginning to realize that he was obviously ignoring her. And she couldn't understand why. He seemed to blow hot and cold every other day it was all very confusing to Mia. She wished he would pick a mood and stick to it. It was driving her crazy constantly wondering why he would be ignoring her. She hadn't done anything besides have sex with him, but he was there, and he showed no signs of stopping it so she honestly couldn't understand him. He could've easily told her to back off, but he had kissed her back. She felt his need and want for her in the kisses they shared.

She had gone to the bar with the Hell Kats so she could have a drink with her new friends and her team. She finally belonged somewhere again and she couldn't be happier. She also needed a distraction because she was constantly consumed by thoughts of Sage, like where he was, why didn't he want to see her, and did he not enjoy having sex with her as much as she had enjoyed being with him? She had been enjoying herself, having a few drinks and dancing with the rest of the Hell Kats. It was the first time in a long time where she felt really happy. She smiled and joked around with the girls. She hadn't expected to see Sage any time soon and especially at the bar so when she saw him walk into the bar, it had thrown her completely off guard. He had been avoiding her for days, and she couldn't deny that her feelings were hurt. Did he just use me for sex, she had asked herself. She knew the sex was great. She had been there and she had felt the chemistry between them. It wasn't lacking passion at all so she couldn't under-stand why he had pulled away from her, and even Sage wouldn't be able to deny the heat that exploded between them.

He's not worth it, she tried to tell herself. She knew she was worth more than that, worth more than just sex. Worth more than being treated like trash.

She was worth more than allowing a man to get under her skin the way she had allowed Sage to and she was definitely worth more than letting a man's actions toward her make her feel less confident within herself. She could not understand why Sage would be so cruel to her. If he wasn't interested, he could've just told her because he was constantly contradicting himself.

He had constantly told her it wasn't going to happen and yet they had slept together a couple of times and every time she could sense it wasn't just physical for either of them. There had to be something more that Sage just wasn't willing to admit. Sage had given in to her just as much as she had given in to him, so she knew she hadn't forced him to do anything. He had been more than willing to get into bed with her both times and even the night they almost slept together for the first time she could tell he wanted her. He always had a burning look in his eyes whenever he looked at her and she could tell.

However, when he saw her as soon as he entered the bar, instead of even acknowledging her, his eyes glazed over her as if she wasn't even standing there, and he continued to just walk straight past her and headed straight for the bar where he greeted all the men at the bar and got himself a drink. Mia couldn't believe it. She had to tell herself not to break down right there in front of everyone. The sting of rejection hit her hard in the chest, and she felt as if he had just ripped her heart out. How could he have seen her in her most vulnerable state and then just chucked her away like rubbish? Tears pricked her eyes and her throat burnt with emotion that had begun to rise to the surface.

She couldn't stand to look at him, and she could not act as if everything was fine. She couldn't stay at the bar any longer as seeing Sage there was just too much. He made her sad and frustrated all at the same time, and that was just way too much emotion to feel all at once, so she decided to say goodbye to the Hell Kats and headed out of the bar. She didn't need him, that was for sure. She wanted to be alone for once. Even though she had been alone for a while, this time it would be by choice.

She hadn't gotten a car yet, and she didn't think it would be a good idea to hop on a bike and ride home since she had had a few drinks before Sage had shown up, so she called for a taxi and went home, wanting to be as far away from Sage as humanly possible. He had ruined her night, and she felt sorry for herself. She shouldn't have allowed him to ruin her night because she was there for herself and not him but what was done was done and she just wanted to think about everything by herself.

She had felt so unbearably alone at the house for so long that she had started to hate the silence that she would often feel enveloped in, but when she got home that night she was thankful for it. She needed to process her thoughts and the best way for her to do that was in silence. She couldn't ever understand why Fiona had gotten the two of them such a big house and with Sage constantly avoiding her, it felt bigger and lonelier every single day. She would often find herself sitting alone at the dinner table, sitting alone in the lounge watching tv. For Mia, it felt as if she was living with a ghost. She sat in her room in silence, thinking over and over again that she should not allow herself to get so emotional over Sage. She could feel the tears threatening to fill her eyes once again, wanting a chance to let go and rush down her cheeks, but Mia wasn't about to let herself cry over a man. You have been through worse things in your life, she told herself, you have no reason to cry over someone who clearly is not good for you. Sage didn't deserve her tears, and she definitely should not shed any because of him.

After she had been sitting in her room for a while, she decided to run a warm bath, filled with bubbles, with candles, some music, and some wine. She wanted to try to calm herself before she went into his room and trashed the place. That was a thought she had had in her mind the whole way home from the club.

She would've gone straight to his room and destroyed it, she would've started with his things in his bathroom. She would've emptied out all of the tubes of product he had, his body wash, his creams, his hair products, shaving cream, toothpaste, everything. She would empty it all into the sink, creating a mess that he could clean up. She would've then moved on and gone into his bedroom. She wouldn't just remove things from shelves. She would cut up his clothes and chuck them everywhere. She would've made holes in all of his shoes.

Her imagination had run wild during her ride home, but she knew she was better than that, so she didn't bother.

She climbed into the bath that she had run herself and submerged herself in the bubbles, downing her already poured glass of wine and then reached for the bottle. She stayed in the bath for a few minutes trying to relax. She closed her eyes and tried to concentrate on the music, but it wasn't working, and soon she got out of the bath and changed into a set of old clothes.

Mia decided this would be the best time to get her art supplies out so she could release her emotions properly while doing something she loved. She hadn't gotten around to using them since she had bought them and she felt that this was as good a time as any. So she took her supplies out of her cupboard and placed them into one of the offices closest to her bedroom. She then moved and covered all the furniture, so she had enough space to lay out her art supplies and to keep the furniture from getting any paint on them in the process because she didn't want to actually damage anything while she found her release. She knew it could get messy depending on how carried away she got, and she had a feeling that she would definitely be getting carried away. Her emotions were at a tipping point.

She had never thought that she would ever feel crazy, crazy enough to want to damage things that weren't hers. She had always managed to keep herself controlled and calm, but she had never felt like this before, and right then she blamed Sage. It was all his fault.

She set up one of the blank canvases she had bought and placed it on an easel. She stared at her tubes of paint for a long while before she reached over and picked up her first color of choice, black. Black suited her emotional state, she was starting to feel empty inside, and she hated it. She knew she was stronger, but she had been bottling up her feelings for far too long, and she could no longer hold them back. If she could, she'd much prefer hitting Sage, calling him names in the process.

She almost covered the entire canvas with black. It started as a blob right in the middle of the canvas, but after she started to work with it, she could see it transforming into something. She reached for her second color of choice, grey. It was clear to her that it was her sadness coming through, she could feel it with every brush stroke. She did not necessarily focus on what she was painting. She just let herself get wrapped up in the movement of the strokes, and before she knew it, she had found a rhythm, painting here and shadowing there. She was consumed. When she decided to take a step back so she could look at what she had painted, she could make out a silhouette had been made with the black paint while she had used the grey to paint the background, then she had mixed the black and grey together causing a contrast. It showed a saddened atmosphere surrounding the silhouette. It made her mad to see how she had lost herself within her emotions. She had always tried to stay strong, but with Sage, she had somehow let herself go. She had let her emotions get the best of her, and now she felt like a stupid teenager who had gotten their heart broken.

She could never understand the effect he had on her. He had gone out of his way to ignore her most of the time, but somehow she had still managed to get wrapped up in him, and he had crept into her mind almost all the time. She felt stupid for ever thinking he could possibly feel the same about her. A part of her wanted to break the canvas. She couldn't bear the frustration she had with herself and Sage.

The longer she stared at the painting, the more frustrated she got so she reached for her paints and picked up the one red she had bought. At the time she had been drawn to it because of how deep it was, and as she painted with it, she couldn't help but be reminded of blood. She was completely enraged at that point, almost making slashing movements on the canvas. In her mind, she was not picturing hurting anyone while she moved her brush, but she was releasing all of her anger, and it felt good to her when she could almost slash through the sadness that she had put on the canvas in front of her. She had to remind herself that she should not be sad. She had to let go of that feeling. In her mind, she was cutting through it, cutting the sadness out of herself. Cutting the emotional wounds open so all her pain would collapse outside of her. She pulled away from the painting, looking at it long and hard. She had gone side to side with the red, some slashes were bigger than others, the biggest one being on the chest of the silhouette. To her, it symbolized her chest, her opening her chest so she could release all the pain and hurt she felt from Sage. He had made her feel so lost and confused but painting had definitely helped to get rid of some of those feelings. She had completely forgotten what it felt like to feel pain again and she soon couldn't understand why she had ever stopped.

She proceeded to pick up a bright yellow tube of paint and as the red slashes were angled from side to side of the canvas, she started to place the yellow in the centers of each symbolic slash, as if to show a bit of light coming through. She knew she could do better and she knew she had to gain more control over her emotions from then onward. She needed to remind herself that through everything she was strong and powerful. She never needed anyone to reassure her of that because she knew it deep down in her heart.

The reason she had always been drawn to painting was because of how it had made her feel. She could always almost instantly feel a difference in herself when she got wrapped up in a painting, letting her mind go completely while her hands did all the work. She hadn't felt so good in a long time and so she decided to pick up a fresh canvas to create another piece as she still felt like she had more emotions pent up inside. She moved the first painting into one corner of the office so it could dry.

The second painting wasn't as dark and wasn't as sad, but she could tell she still had sadness in her heart and she wasn't sure if that would go away until the situation between her and Sage had been resolved. She needed to hear from his own mouth exactly what was going on between them because the guessing game was definitely not working for her. Her emotions were already too involved, and she wanted to know if the feelings were at all mutual.

In her head, she had come to believe that they weren't mutual due to the way Sage had been treating her recently, but she couldn't understand why he had shared a bed with her, why he had had sex with her if she meant nothing to him. Mia wasn't the type of girl who slept with just anyone and Sage must've known that. *Why would he take advantage of her like that?* she thought to herself.

Sage also knew that she had had a hard life, mostly caused by herself but nevertheless it didn't change the fact that, out of all people, Sage should show her more respect than he had lately. She had shared her life story with him. He knew almost all her flaws and faults. He should've been kinder to her. He should've been honest and stuck to his word if he didn't want anything to happen between the two of them.

Mia tried not to focus on Sage anymore as she continued to paint, and the more she painted, the better she felt. She knew she should paint more often, especially when her head started getting all confused. She thought about why her parents didn't want her to be an artist when she was younger, and it was probably because they could never understand the feelings she was trying to portray. She knew it was hard for people to understand the emotions of someone else when that person had no experience with the same feelings. She knew she was talented all those years ago, and she knew she was still talented now. She just didn't have anyone who understood her. She thought no one would ever be able to understand her. Sometimes she struggled to understand herself. She often thought about her life and how it would've been if she had started with her parents and while she was painting, she couldn't help but feel a little vulnerable.

Once she had completed three paintings, she stared at the differences between them, each one of them getting lighter with more grey and less black, as well as the red and yellow mixed together to create an orange halo of light. She could deal with that for now. She headed to her bathroom for a shower. She was a messy painter, and so she had managed to get paint in her hair, on her face, under her nails and a little bit on her clothes. She would have to look into getting some overalls so she wouldn't ruin any more clothes because she knew she would continue to paint whenever she could.

She got into a hot, steaming shower, rinsing off the paint and the feelings of the day. She stood in the shower for a while just letting the water rush over her, picturing it cleansing her from her head to her feet, and on some level she pictured it cleansing her heart and soul. She washed herself until her body stung. She felt that the harder she rubbed her skin, the better she felt, as if she were new again. After stepping out of the shower, she patted herself dry, got dressed in fresh pajamas, and decided to make herself a cup of tea before she headed to bed. She would've tried to stay up and wait for Sage like she normally did, but she decided not to waste her time, and so she climbed into bed and soon fell asleep dreaming of Sage because even in her sleep she couldn't stop thinking about him.

*"I love you, Mia," said Sage.*

*She knew she couldn't deny that she loved him too. She had been denying it within herself for so long that she knew she just wanted the words to fall out of her mouth. Just like a river had no control over the water that flowed through it, Mia had no control over her feelings for Sage.*

*"I love you too," she replied with a goofy grin plastered on her face. Sage looked so angelic, his brown hair flowing around his head, creating a halo effect. Mia felt extremely happy in that moment. Sage had told her he loved her, and now they could finally be together, like she had always wanted.*

*Sage took her hands and intertwined his fingers with hers.*

*"I'm so glad you feel the same way. Everything has been so messed up, and I couldn't stand it any longer. I knew I had to tell you just how I felt before I ran the risk of losing you for good. I'm so sorry for all the pain I've caused you. I was only trying to protect you," he said with a sad expression on his beautiful face.*

*" Shh, it's alright. I can understand where you were coming from so we can only work on a better future for the two of us," Mia replied as she gently brushed her fingers across his cheek, feeling his freshly shaven face beneath her fingers.*

*Sage kissed her softly on her lips, and a smile broke across her face. Her heart felt like it could leave her chest.*

She slept that night with a smile on her face, completely captivated by her dream and how real it felt. Mia continued to sleep peacefully, slipping in and out of different dreams that all had Sage in them.

*It was 5 years later. Mia was sitting on a porch swing in the middle of winter. She had a scarf wrapped around her* neck, gloves placed tight on her hands, and she had winter boots on that had thick woolen socks underneath. She was gently swinging back and forth as she sat quite still on the swing. Her arms were wrapped around her body, trying to keep the cold in and although she had slowly started to freeze she couldn't get herself to move. The garden that lay before her was so mesmerizing she could stare at it all day.

"Honey, what are you doing outside? It's freezing!" a voice said from behind her. She turned around and laid her eyes upon Sage. He looked even better than he did five years ago, she thought.

"I'm just taking in the view," she replied as she pointed to the snow-covered garden, "Isn't it beautiful?" she asked.

"Why, yes, it is beautiful, but your beautiful little nose is going to freeze and fall off of your face soon!" he exclaimed. She laughed. He would always remind her of her beauty even when she felt like she was constantly looking at a demi-god whenever she looked at him.

"Oh hush," she said as she waved a hand at him, dismissing his compliment.

"Will you come sit with me for a while before we head inside?" she asked him. A smile grew across his face.

"Me? Sit next to a Queen?" he asked with a wink. She laughed again. The one thing she had loved about him was his constant sense of humor that always brought a smile to her face no matter what mood she was in.

"Yes, a King does tend to take his place next to his Queen," she replied playfully.

He sat down next to her, wrapping his arm around her shoulders. She leaned her head and nested it in the hollow of his neck, and the two of them sat quietly outside in the winter cold staring at the snow-covered garden.

"Isn't it beautiful?" she asked again.

"Yes, my dear. It most certainly is," he replied.

ia had woken up disappointed. Not only had she dreamt of Sage, but the dream had left a sore pang in her chest. It had felt so real that when she woke up, she half expected Sage to be in bed next to her, but sadly she was alone, again. Even after the night before she couldn't shake the need and want she had for him. She just wanted to know if he felt the same way at all. The dream left a longing in her chest. She longed for Sage in a way that was stronger than she had before.

She knew Sage didn't love her and he probably hadn't even pictured a future with her. She hated that it was possible for her to love him regardless. He had hurt her, but she still couldn't stop herself from feeling the way she did. She hated herself for it. When had she become so weak, she had to ask herself. She had always been a strong person when it came to men so she couldn't understand what it was about Sage; she just couldn't get over him. She had tried to look after him, and he never showed her any gratitude. He seemed to ignore her any chance he got, and to Mia, she just couldn't understand why she'd want someone like that. She knew she deserved better and any woman would agree with her and yet she still found herself wanting and needing Sage. As much as she told herself to feel otherwise, she could not. Her mind and heart were apparently completely consumed by him.

She wished the situation weren't so damned hard, but she knew she couldn't get everything she wished for. She wanted to bury herself in her bed. Staying there would definitely not make the situation easier because it would still be there when she got up, but it meant she wouldn't have to face anyone, especially Sage. She wasn't sure she could face him after the night before and especially after her dream. It had left her in a state of embarrassment because even after everything he had done to her she still dreamt of him, and she wanted that dream to be so much more than just a dream. She felt betrayed by herself for wanting him. How could she want a man who showed her no respect, who constantly made her feel less of herself?

When she was growing up, she pictured the man she would end up with, not by his looks but by his character and by what she had seen. She knew she wanted a man who would always be there for her no matter what, who wanted to be there for her when she got confused about life so they could work through it together and come out better together as well as individuals. She wanted a man who would love her despite all her flaws. She wanted someone who could see straight through them and think of them as things that made her who she was rather than used them against her to make her feel less than worthy. She wanted a man who she could see herself having children with, someone who would be there for them no matter what. And when she had first met Sage, she thought it would be him. He was so kind and gentle with her in the beginning, treating her with respect and compassion. She thought back to the night she had shared her life story with him. He had been a completely different person back then and she couldn't help but wish that the person she had met back then would come back now; because the person he had become wasn't the man she had met and she knew it.

Although Sage has been avoiding her, Mia had always been able to tell when he had been home because she had taken on the responsibility of cleaning up around the house. After all, it was mostly Mia who would actually eat at the house, alone, while Sage was out at work. When she cooked the first night he didn't come home for dinner. She had made extra for him, so at least he wouldn't starve, but she noticed he hadn't bothered eating it, so she threw it away and didn't bother cooking for him again. She was trying to make the living situation easier for both of them, making sure that he was still eating properly, but he made her feel like her efforts were pointless.

He had almost completely changed toward her. He had always tried to keep his distance and she knew that but avoiding and ignoring her on a day to day basis was taking it a little too far. How could he just switch off completely toward her, she thought. Had there been an alien invasion she didn't know about, had he been switched during the day and she had been left with a heartless creature instead of the man she thought she knew? It was highly unlikely, but she preferred to think it possible just to make herself feel a little better about the situation at hand. She remembered that he had been in the army so it was possible for him to remove himself emotionally at a whim. Having a history like that, she knew he would be able to switch off, but she found it hard to believe considering it had come out of nowhere.

She would start her day by making her bed, and on that day she decided to change her sheets as well so when she went to bed in the evening, she could sleep on fresh sheets and picture it as a clean place to place her head while she slept. She wouldn't say she was spiritual but she did believe that bad energy and bad feelings could linger in items of clothing and linen. After she was done changing her sheets and making her bed, she headed for the shower. She put the radio on in the background with some nice, upbeat music to keep her in a good mood. Today would be a good day she told herself. She always felt like she could be more productive if she showered before she started her day properly. She then headed to the kitchen after she had finished getting ready, she would usually clean up any mess in the kitchen left by Sage when he made himself coffee before heading out for the day. He wouldn't eat her food but he sure as hell didn't care that she had to clean up after him. Sometimes she noticed that he wouldn't make coffee so it wasn't unusual to see the kitchen clean. Mia entered the clean kitchen and didn't think anything of it and proceeded to make herself breakfast. Growing up, her mother had always told her that breakfast was the most important meal of the day, and so she had always continued to start her day with a full and healthy breakfast.

*"You have to remember, Mia, your body has been asleep for 8 hours or so and it's very important for you to have breakfast when you wake up in the morning. Your body needs it to function. It's like you've been a bear in hibernation, and obviously, the first thing they do when they wake up is eat and so should you!" her mother told her as she handed her a plate filled with pancakes, fruit, and bacon.*

"But I'm not a bear, mother, I'm an ordinary human who doesn't always feel hungry in the morning," Mia had stated as she stared at the huge plate of food before her. She had no idea how she could finish it all, but she knew her mother wouldn't let her leave the table if she didn't, even if it meant she would be late for school.

"You may not feel hungry, but you need to eat," her mother said as she eyed her from across the table. She picked up her coffee and took a sip. She also would not leave the table until Mia was done. She was trapped and had to eat; she didn't have any other choice.

"Yes, mother, I know," Mia replied with a roll of her eyes as she picked up her knife and fork and slowly started to tackle the plate that had been placed in front of her. She would deny it to anyone who asked, but the minute she got a piece of fruit or pancake in her mouth, she would salivate, and she'd realize that she was, in fact, hungry after all.

Her mother harped on with just about anything. 'You need to do this, and you need to do that,' she would say. Constantly drilling things into Mia's head over the years. It was honestly no wonder despite everything else Mia wanted to leave her home at such a young age. Her parents drove her mad when it came to just about anything.

Although Mia loved her mother, she had always hated how much she would try to control her because, even after all the years, there were still things Mia had to do because she didn't know how not to do them due to her mother's constant instruction. She supposed it had definitely made her house trained. She had learned a lot from her mother about housekeeping too, and she should be grateful for that.

That morning she made herself scrambled eggs on toast with bacon and a cup of coffee. She sat at the dining table by herself and slowly ate her breakfast. Although she had woken up with a pang of disappointment, she was glad that most of the sadness from the night before had left her mind and her heart. She could possibly face the day and be alright. She had left the music on from her bedroom, and she could softly hear it traveling throughout the house. She could feel herself getting lighter and lighter, ready to face whatever the day brought her way. She slowly started to hum along to the music while she ate, feeling the positive vibrations travel through her body. She would have started dancing if she had allowed herself, but she knew she should take it easy since it was only the morning. She continued to sit at the dining room table just a little bit longer before she decided to get on with her day. She wanted to make sure her food had settled in her stomach for a bit before she became too active. She always knew the importance of allowing a meal to settle first so the body could start digesting it before moving too much. She had suffered from a lot of stomach problems growing up because she was always too quick to move after eating.

She preferred to clean up as she went so she wouldn't have to backtrack throughout the house to clean up any mess that had been left behind and so after she was done with breakfast she washed her dishes, dried them and carefully placed them back into their designated areas.

She then cleaned the rest of the kitchen before she headed to Sage's room. She was luckily the only one who really cooked in the kitchen so besides some of the mess from breakfast, there wasn't much mess for Mia to clean.

She proceeded to his room to check if he had any laundry because she did that on a daily basis when it came to both his and her clothes. It was just easier than letting them pile up for too long. She noticed his bed hadn't been slept in. She would know considering she had made his bed the day before as she did most mornings. She found it rather odd that he hadn't slept in his bed. Had he slept on the couch maybe, she wondered, maybe he had too much to drink at the bar and couldn't make it to his bed when he had gotten home.

Living with Sage had been a big adjustment for Mia because she had never lived with anyone before, let alone a guy. Because it was just the two of them, she didn't feel it necessary for them to get a maid, so she ended up cleaning up after him a lot. She didn't mind so much because he was quite a neat person, clearly from all his army training. Only occasionally would he forget to clean up after himself, like leaving his bed unmade, whereas Mia had always made her bed when she woke up in the mornings.

Next she went into his bathroom to check if the shower had been used. She could always tell because the smell of his body wash and cologne always lingered in the air after every shower he took, and to her surprise, the bathroom was neat and had no evidence that it had been used recently. She definitely found it strange as no matter what he would always come home, and he would always have a shower before he went anywhere. He seemed to be a hygiene freak in that aspect, she had noticed. He would rarely go to work without a shower, and sometimes he'd take a second shower when he got home from work.

It was a guilty pleasure of Mia's to sit in his bathroom long after he had left and just breathe in the body wash and cologne that still hung in the air. To her, it was almost the same as smelling someone's clothes when you missed them and she definitely missed Sage and being around him. She hadn't managed to break down his guard completely, but she always felt at ease around him, and she wouldn't have minded just being able to sit next to him. She missed the smell of him that morning.

Mia knew there could be many reasons why he hadn't come home, especially since he worked for Grier and the Screaming Demons, but he would usually tell her if he was doing any business after hours. He had at least always been thoughtful about her waiting up for him and it was still completely out of character for him to not come home at all, she thought. She knew he liked sleeping in his own bed.

The Screaming Demons were usually pretty clean when it came to business around the chop shop, mostly using stuff that was safe. Besides, having people who might want to steal the merchandise, everything normally ran smoothly without a hitch. Mia knew there were things being done behind closed doors that no one really talked about, stuff that could get people like Sage into a lot of trouble. She had never liked the idea of the things he had to do for Grier but who was she to tell him not to do it? Definitely no one of interest to him.

It was highly unlikely that he could've been caught. He had been involved for so long that Mia knew that Sage knew what he was doing, but anything could be possible. Mia couldn't help but think that something bad had gone down after she had left the bar the night before. It didn't make sense to her for him to do something that night though. He never drank on the job even when it was after hours. Had Sage done some side business after hours either way and gotten caught, she asked herself. She didn't know what to think, and only the worst things came to her mind. If Sage had gotten caught, he could be in jail, and she wouldn't even know considering she doubted he would call her. He'd probably call Grier who may or may not inform Mia of the situation. She couldn't help but be stressed out as the day started to tick by.

Had Sage maybe spent the night with someone else, she wondered. It would explain why he had ignored her. He had probably gotten tired of her and was ready for the next person. Although it was painful to think about, it would be a lot easier to come to terms with than Sage being behind bars. She tried calling his phone, but it went straight to voicemail. She knew then that something had gone wrong. She felt it in her gut, and she knew her gut had always been right in the past. She didn't know what to think nor what to do. Should she call the police station herself and see if they had him or should she just wait it out, she wondered. She had never been in a situation like this before. Dealing with a missing person was serious and in their line of work she didn't think it would be a good idea to get the police involved, especially since they were both new to town. Besides asking questions within the Screaming Demons, she didn't know what else she could do that wouldn't cause any trouble. If her gut instinct was right, she needed to find out where Sage was as soon as possible.

## 16

Mia spent the day trying to distract herself. She had started asking around the bar if anyone knew where Sage was, but no one had answers which caused alarm bells to go off in her head. No one said that there was an outside job that he needed to do the night before, so she crossed that off of her list of possible reasons for his absence. She tried to keep her thoughts at bay, but until Sage returned, her mind could not be settled. She had tried to call him more than once, but each time there was no answer, the call would just go straight to voicemail. His phone had clearly been switched off. Had he gone off the radar for a while? However, that was highly unlikely. He couldn't risk missing a call from Grier or Fiona, considering they called him every couple of days to check on things. Mia knew he respected Grier so him ditching work and his phone just didn't make sense to her.

She had originally thought he could be with another woman, but soon that idea left her mind. It had taken her so long to get him to let her in, and even then he hadn't let her in completely. She couldn't imagine he would be with anyone else so quickly after her when he had tried to fight her off for so long. And even though he had proven to be a different person than she thought she had met, she knew that was something he wouldn't do. She had heard him screaming out Laura's name while he slept, and of course, she knew exactly who Laura was. She knew that he would never be able to completely let her go after what had happened. It wasn't within his control. She could definitely tell that he didn't seem like the type of man to just go off with a woman he had met at a bar. Knowing this just made Mia stress even more because she had no other ideas as to where he could be. It just didn't make sense for him to just disappear. Obviously though, if that were the case, she wouldn't be able to stop him from doing anything with anyone else. She didn't own him, and he certainly had made his feelings clear the last time she saw him.

His clothes were still in his cupboard, so it was evident that he hadn't decided to move out. Fiona would go crazy if he tried something like that and Mia doubted that Sage would try to cause any bad blood considering he enjoyed working for Fiona and Grier. She knew he loved his job because he had always prided himself in giving his best and giving his all when it came to every job Grier gave him. Everyone knew he had a troubled past so they could see him trying to make himself better by constantly trying to prove himself to those around him, especially Grier and now Fiona. Mia felt the same way he did about it. She knew she had a lot to prove and she had a big sign hanging over her head that read 'Kick me out if I screw up.' She had been trying her best, but now she was worried that something had gone terribly wrong and she had no control over the situation because she didn't understand what was going on.

Without wanting to jump the gun and cause any unnecessary concern, she decided to wait one more day before she took any action. He could still turn up as if there were nothing to be concerned about in the first place. She wouldn't be surprised if that did happen. It all seemed like some sick joke to her and she really just wanted Sage to come home.

She went to bed stressed out. She tossed and turned the entire night, constantly waking up thinking she had heard something in the house or someone coming in, but she was always wrong and had fallen back to sleep every time. She went to bed hoping that she was just overthinking and that soon Sage would come home to her. Well, not come home to her exactly but just for him to come home in general.

On the second day, she tried to keep herself busy, but her mind wouldn't have it. She stayed at the house waiting to see if he turned up in the evening after possibly staying the night at a hotel and going straight to work after that. She continued to ask around at the bar and still no answers. She waited up for him that night, again constantly praying he would just come through the doors. But still, he hadn't been seen or heard from.

Her feeling of unease just kept growing when she discovered that Sage hadn't come home the second night. She had gotten out of bed without making it and rushed to Sage's room, and again she found his bed neat like she had left it two days ago and so she decided to call Fiona. She couldn't keep Sage's unknown whereabouts to herself and she knew that if anyone could track him down it would be Fiona and Grier. It was time to get all hands on deck so they could find out exactly where Sage was. She couldn't wait any longer. She didn't know if he was dead or alive and every passing minute could determine whether or not they found him in one piece and still breathing.

On the second ring, Fiona picked up. Mia was so scared to tell her the situation, she honestly didn't know how she would react. Would she get mad that Mia had left it so long or would she understand why she had waited a few days?

"Hello, Mia. How is everything going down there?" she asked.

"Um, hi, Fiona, everything seems to be going well…" Mia said. She was unsure about how to explain the situation. She knew she needed to get to the point because she was driving herself insane, being the only one concerned.

"What do you mean everything seems to be going well? That doesn't sound so certain," Fiona replied.

"Well, I'm actually calling because no one has heard from Sage for two days now. Obviously, that's very out of character of him since he usually always comes home, so I'm starting to get a little concerned. I know I've left it a few days before telling you, but I wanted to make sure I wasn't overreacting," she said.

"Do you know the last place he was seen?" Fiona asked with concern in her voice. "I completely understand why you waited, and you don't need to explain that to me. Dealing with something like this is always difficult because until we find him and find out what has happened, it could turn out to be a misunderstanding," Fiona also said. Mia was grateful that Fiona had understood her. She didn't want to get in trouble when she had been going out of her mind with concern for Sage's wellbeing. Fiona had sent Sage out with Mia to protect her as both of them took over the Screaming Demons in Florida. Fiona was definitely concerned because although he had complained about going to Florida with Mia, he had agreed because he followed instructions very well.

"Yes, he was at the bar the last time he was seen." The same night he had ignored her, she wished more than anything she had spoken to him, maybe if she had he wouldn't be missing. Maybe talking to him could have changed how things played out that night, maybe he would've gone home with her instead of staying at the bar.

"Did anything happen out of the ordinary?" Fiona asked, trying to get as much information as possible.

"I heard there was a scene caused by a member of the Omens who had entered the bar. But I wasn't there, so I'm not entirely sure what actually happened."

The story that had been told to Mia was that one of the members from the Omens had gone into the bar and caused a scene, Sage got the best of him, and the man was beaten almost to death but let go. Mia didn't want to tell Fiona the story because she was worried that Sage's actions would get him in trouble with the big boss when he did eventually turn up, and she didn't want to be the cause of that. Mia knew Sage shouldn't have let the guy go, everyone knew better than that; she couldn't understand why he had been so soft. He knew how those kinds of things went. It was just no good sending a message to the leader of the Omens when it was clear they wanted revenge for Tyler. Sage knew he should've ended it then and there, and Mia knew she would have to find out from him why he had let him go.

"Okay, well I'm going to send Grier there. He'll come by plane so he can get there as soon as possible, and hopefully he can get some answers. Mia, until he arrives, I want you to stay in the house. We don't know what we're dealing with here and I don't want you to be in any sort of danger," Fiona said.

"Oh, great, okay, yes. I'll stay in the house until he arrives." Mia was pleased to hear that Grier would be coming to help figure out exactly what was going on, but Mia knew that if it came to it, she would do whatever it took to find Sage, even if she went without Grier.

"Great, I'll get him to contact you once he's landed so you know to expect him."

"Thank you, Fiona, I'll be in contact with you soon," Mia said, and then the line went dead.

Mia knew that Fiona had grown to trust her since she had moved to Florida. She had been her eyes and ears within the new Hell Kats and over time, Fiona learned that Mia had been trying her best to prove she could be trusted again within the business. Mia had been reporting anything and everything she could that would be important to Fiona.

She stayed at the house, constantly going around to every window and every door making sure everything was locked. She had no idea what was going on, and she knew she could be the next target if anything had happened to Sage. She knew it would take a couple of hours before Grier arrived and so she sat in the lounge closest to the main door so that she could let him in the minute he arrived, but when the doorbell rang out throughout the house a few minutes after she had ended her call with Fiona, she couldn't help but feel extremely scared and vulnerable. Had someone come after her now, had they rung the bell to tease her, was her house surrounded by Omens? Every question imaginable sprung to her mind. She was all alone, she was defenseless without Sage.

The doorbell had a camera just above it, so Mia went to the monitor to check who was at the door. She could see the face of a man who looked familiar, but she couldn't remember who he was. She didn't know if she should even bother talking to the man; she was scared.

She decided to use the intercom to communicate with him before she dared to open the door for him. Maybe he had something important to tell her, maybe it was a demand from the Omens, a ransom price so she could get Sage back.

"Hello? Who's there?" she asked. Her voice sounded weak as it echoed back to her throughout her house.

"Hi, Mia? It's Mike from the bar. I've been put in charge of the bar remember, we met a few nights ago, I was behind the bar the night Sage went missing," he explained. His face was almost out of the camera's view as he had leaned forward to reply to her, but Mia could remember seeing his face when she had gone into the bar just days before.

"Yes. I remember you. Can I help you with anything?" she was still hesitant to let him in.

"Well, I was hoping you'd let me in so I could talk to you face to face. It's about Sage."

At the mention of Sage, she immediately started unlocking the front door. If he had any information for her, she needed to hear it as soon as possible.

She swung open the front door, and Mike greeted her with an extended hand. She shook it and soon showed him into the house, making sure to lock the door behind her just in case. She couldn't be too safe now that she was on her own and unsure of what was going on.

"Please come in. Can I offer you anything to drink?" she asked. As much as she wanted the information he came with, she could not be rude. She had also been taught to always offer guests a beverage, again another lesson learned from her mother.

"No, ma'am, I'm alright. Thank you," he said with a gentle smile. Mia instantly trusted him. She could tell from his face that he meant no harm to her. He looked like a gentleman, roughly around his early to mid 30's she'd assume. He had a few grey hairs showing through around his beard and littered throughout his hair. She could sense he was very nervous and possibly scared of sharing the information he had. Mia only hoped it would be the information that she needed to find Sage.

"Oh, please, don't call me ma'am. That's what you'd call my grandmother," she replied. "Please take a seat," she said as she led him into the lounge she had been sitting in before his arrival. She was a little glad she had a bit of company, even under the circumstances. The empty house felt haunting when she was alone.

She took a seat and gestured to the couch in front of her for Mike to sit on.

"Thank you," he said as he took the seat opposite her.

After a few minutes of awkward silence, Mia had to ask the question that hung in the air.

"What information can you give me?" she asked him. She couldn't take the pleasantries anymore. If he had something he wanted to share, she needed to know, as time was ticking by.

"Well, I heard that you were asking about Sage's whereabouts, so I took it upon myself to look at the footage from the night he was at the bar, his last known location. I remember he had a few whiskeys before he left so I thought it was possible that he could've gone to a hotel near the bar instead of him heading home, you know, just in case he felt unable to drive," Mike stated. Mia nodded, she knew Sage was very responsible when it came to drinking and driving so it could've been possible.

"And what did you find when you looked at the footage?" Mia asked. She really just wanted him to get to the point so she could find Sage.

"I looked at the footage from the camera we have located outside the bar, and I'm sorry to inform you, but it appears that Sage was jumped when he exited the bar. It would seem that two men attacked him and then put him in the back of a black vehicle before they drove off," he said with a very serious face. Mia's worst nightmare had just come true. She didn't want to believe it. How could this be happening? She suddenly felt a bit dizzy, so she leaned forward and rested her head between her hands while her elbows rested on her knees.

"No, no, no. This can't be happening," she said out loud as her emotions tipped over and out of her mouth before she could do anything to stop herself. She had been in emotional hell for the past few days so it was completely understandable that her emotions had slipped to the surface without any warning. Mike sat in silence as he watched Mia process the information he had given her.

Mia could not believe what she had heard. Sage was

taken. He was taken two days ago, and if he was in the hands of the Omens who she instantly thought were behind it all, she had no idea if he would still be alive. She hated herself for staying mad at him even while she had been concerned. If he weren't alive, she would not be able to live with herself.

"Could you make out anything about the men?" she asked as calmly as she could. She couldn't break down, at least not until she was alone.

"Yes, they were wearing the Omens cut." The minute he said it, Mia knew it could only mean serious danger. Shit, she thought, the situation was definitely worse than she had thought, and if it were possible, she almost wished Sage had run off with someone else instead of being trapped somewhere.

"Damn it. Okay, I need that footage. Can you get it for me?" she asked. She would need to look at it herself and find out if anyone could help her identify the men. Without a word, Mike took out a see-through square plastic case that had a DVD enveloped inside from inside his jacket pockets.

"I thought you'd want it immediately," he said as he handed it over to her. He was prepared, and Mia was grateful for that because she needed to get stuck in so she could find exactly who had taken Sage and work their way to locating him.

"Thank you so much," she replied as she took the DVD from him.

"I'm happy to help, and please let me know if there is anything else I can assist you with," he said as he got up and headed for the door.

"I will do that."

After showing him out, she was relieved that she would soon figure out who was responsible for taking Sage and make them pay.

She thought it would be a good idea to call Fiona, so she knew about the situation, but when Mia called, she didn't pick up. She decided to leave a message.

*"Hi, Fiona. It's Mia. The bartender who worked the night Sage disappeared has just been over. He informed me of the worst-case scenario, Sage has been taken by the Omens. I have the footage from the attack that happened outside the bar. I'll be going through it to figure out who took him and how we can get him back. I'll keep you updated."*

## 17

Sage had been trapped for at least two days, but he couldn't be sure exactly how long because he couldn't see the sun. He had been starved, having only water to survive on. He did not know how much longer he could go without food. He had been trained in the army to survive any sort of attack and short periods of starvation but he knew his body wasn't strong enough to withstand this amount of starvation. After all, he wasn't Superman. He hadn't eaten much the day they got him either, so he didn't have a lot stored in his body before they started starving him. He was grateful that they hadn't done anything else to him as he wasn't sure if he'd have been able to survive with all the other injuries his body was trying to heal.

He hadn't gotten much light due to something being placed over the top of the well, so it was hard for him to tell the time. He managed to get glimmers of light that shone in through small cracks throughout the day but other than that, he hadn't seen much light since they trapped him. He could make out the color change in the sky whenever he looked through the cracks which is why he thought it had only been two days. It could, however, have been more. They had destroyed his phone so no one could track his whereabouts. They had covered all their tracks, and Sage knew that it could mean the end of the line for him. He didn't know if anyone would've thought about trying to find him though. Had Mia even realized he was missing? He thought it was doubtful. After all, he had been making his existence in the house almost nonexistent. If no one came for him, he wouldn't blame her. He hadn't exactly been the best person lately.

The water in the well was quite low so it only reached his knees. He was grateful for that but if he were to fall into the water at any point he knew he wouldn't have the strength to keep himself afloat so he'd probably drown. If he thought about it, while he was growing up he had been a little terrified of water because of its unpredictability and he was now in a situation where he might die in a well. He chuckled cruelly at himself. Look at the mess you've gotten yourself in, he whispered to himself.

His whole life seemed pretty futile now that it was

coming to an end. What had he really accomplished in his life? Nothing he could really be proud of. Sure, he had served his country but he hadn't saved anyone. He lost his entire team and he had never been the same since. He hadn't allowed himself to get close to anyone. He had even started pushing his family away over the years. It was not just the nightmares that kept him up at night, but it was also the fact that he didn't deserve to survive. He hadn't made his life worth anything. He should've done more, been more and he supposed it was a good thing someone had taken it upon themselves to now end his life like it should've ended all those years ago.

Where would his teammates be if they had survived, he asked himself. He probably would've married Laura. God knows he wanted to marry her as soon as they got back from Afghanistan. He suspected that the rest of his team would've continued to serve their country, constantly going into dangerous situations and places to protect the lives of the innocent. He couldn't say much for himself, because Sage knew he wouldn't have gone back. It had taken a toll on him regardless of being the only survivor. He would never be able to forget what had happened while he was out on his mission, the people he had killed and the blood he had spilled. His teammates had deserved to live more than he had. In that moment he would've traded his life for theirs. They would have made the world a better place. He definitely knew he wasn't making the world a better place, but maybe it would be better off without him. Dark thoughts started to consume his mind, and soon he was engulfed in a whole lot of self-pity and angst.

He couldn't imagine how his life would be any good to anyone. He remembered all the pain he had caused to people that didn't deserve it, specifically Mia. How he wished he could see her face one last time with her dimples and smile spread across her face like she deserved it to be. He was no good for her. All he had done was cause her unnecessary pain.

He really didn't want to think about dying though because he had already started to freak out more than he wanted to. But at the same time his mind was filled with last wishes and things he wished he could've done differently, like how he couldn't remember the last time he had spoken to his mother or his father, how had he been so cruel to them. They had always wanted the best for him and they had supported everything he did in his life. Even when he had been confused as a young adult and had wasted a few years before deciding to join the army, they supported him. He wished he could be back at home in his old family house surrounded by his family, with everyone crowded around the dining room table, laughing and joking as he watched on.

He allowed himself a moment to think of how it

would be if he had a future with Mia. He could picture her face next to his in multiple photographs lining the shelf that rested above a fireplace. He could picture the both of them curled up in front of it on cold winter nights with a fire roaring in front of them, a Christmas tree in the corner beautifully decorated by Mia with presents laying beneath it for them and the family that they shared. He knew their children would be beautiful, not because of him but because of her. She had a beauty that radiated from deep within, and he couldn't deny that he had seen it the minute he had met her. He would never get a chance with her now, it was all too late. They would never have children. In fact, he realized he would not have children with anyone. His fate had been made, and he didn't stand a chance. He longed to be at home in his bed. A bed would be great right now he thought to himself. He pictured himself sinking into a soft mattress with dozens of warm fluffy blankets covering him from the harsh cold. He couldn't be sure if thinking about being warm helped him or not because his body sent a shiver down his spine.

He had to stop thinking so much. He told himself to get a grip. Soon he passed out, his body constantly sending a shock of pain through him. It was becoming harder and harder to stay awake.

* * *

HE WOKE up when he felt water splash all over his face and body, sending him into a state of shock. He screamed out in pain. His body felt like it was covered in pins and needles. His clothes were wet through, despite the water only reaching knee level. The Omens constantly splashed water on him whenever they paid him a visit but not only that, he had also urinated on himself as he had no other option. He felt disgusting and dirty. He thought that they were probably trying to make him sick so his body would soon turn against him and slowly start to kill him from the inside out and he could slowly feel that starting to happen as he had started getting hot flushes. He'd been quite a healthy person most of his life, but even he couldn't fight anything that happened within him. He tried to will his body to stay calm and fight. He tried to keep his mind busy so he wouldn't go insane. Being trapped in a well with no one to talk to had started to make him talk to himself a little too much, and soon he was worried he'd start replying to himself as if there were someone else there with him.

Sage knew that the well was in the middle of nowhere. He hadn't heard any sort of car traffic pass by. The Omens only came to give him one small cup of water every couple of hours or maybe once a day, he wasn't sure, clearly enjoying the torture they were putting him through. He couldn't hear anyone when he was left alone. He tried calling out to anyone who might hear him, anyone who could help him, but he learned that his cries for help were pointless when no one came for him. He must've been hidden extremely far away from any house and hidden well if no one had found him yet. He clearly wasn't in an area people would go to so he wasn't surprised. The Omens obviously wanted him dead if they had gone through the trouble of making sure he was literally hidden in a secret place. If he thought about it, he was probably hidden on Omens property. It would make perfect sense, he thought. No one would dare go that far out unless they belonged or were looking for trouble. He knew that was the truth because it was the same with the Screaming Demons. No one would ever enter their clubs if they didn't belong there. The Screaming Demons weren't the same as the Omens and Sage knew that. The Omens were evil and cruel people.

The hunger he was going through was slowly starting to rip through his body causing him pain every so often. He couldn't remember the last time he had starved himself and he honestly didn't think he would ever put his body through anything like that again.

He could already slowly feel that his body had shrunk in size as his body started processing his muscles as a way to stay alive. He knew he didn't have much fat stored in his body as he had always remained fit and lean due to his job and the army. He thought now that it wouldn't have been such a bad idea for him not to be so hard on himself while training. He knew that if he had just a little bit more fat percentage his body could survive longer. He could feel cramps starting to take over his body the longer he hung there in the middle of the well. His stomach felt like it had begun to eat itself from the inside and slowly his muscles started going into spasm. He'd cry out in pain only to be unheard by anyone. The cramps were starting to escalate and soon he had spasms running up his legs as his muscles started to fight against him. He passed out yet again.

HE WOULD DO anything just to get out of the well, he thought when he woke up again, but he knew he didn't have much strength left. Maybe the Omens will kill me soon, he thought to himself and he would be lying if he said that a part of him just wanted to die already. The army had made him tough. He had been strong and smart in gun battles but he had never been in a situation like this before. He had never been a religious person so he found it extremely ironic when he started to pray for help. It seemed like the only thing he could do. He didn't want to die, maybe he could turn his life around. Maybe he could do things differently from now on, he just needed a chance. He needed someone to save him because for once in his life, he knew he wasn't able to save himself like all the times before. He was skilled in saving his own skin, he had done it so many times before. He had gotten into so many useless fights when he was growing up, and he had always managed to come out on top. Although he had been blessed with a lean body most of his life, he knew he was smarter than most people when he was growing up, and so he was easily picked on. Maybe that's why he had joined the army. He wanted to save people from things that threatened their life. He knew all too well what it had felt like to be helpless and scared of people. Maybe he had become the bully himself.

So many questions constantly filled his head the more delirious he became.

He had to admit to himself that he knew why he was there, and if he could go back in time he would've made sure that the Omen punk who had walked into the bar a few days ago did not leave and if he survived he would make sure he paid for what he had caused Sage to go through. He knew at the time it was a stupid idea to just let him get away with just a few bruises. Sage should have finished him, but he had been too distracted, and one would say too kind that night by letting him go, and he was paying for it. He could have blamed Mia for distracting him that night, for being a thought that hadn't left his mind right from the start when they first met but he knew he was responsible for what happened and no one else. Mia wasn't even there when the scene broke out in the bar. Sage had only himself to blame even though he would rather be able to point the finger at someone else. He knew better than that.

Instead of letting the guy go with a warning to the rest of the Omens, he should have made him regret entering the bar at all, made sure he didn't leave with a heartbeat but was rather disposed of. It was certainly too late to wish for a different outcome all things considered, but Sage knew that if anything happened again, he would have to finish it. He worked for the Screaming Demons after all and to them, they never left a job unfinished the way he had.

It was as he was leaving the bar for the night, thinking Mia would already be asleep so he could creep back into the house without having to see her again. He didn't want to have to see her face again, especially after what he had done. He got jumped just outside the bar doors when he had his head bent over his phone, so he could dial for a taxi instead of driving himself home. They had come out of the darkness and attacked him, one hitting him on the back of his head with what he could only assume was a baseball bat and the other hitting him behind the knees so he fell completely to the floor unable to defend himself. They hadn't done anything else to him, which had surprised him, but he could tell that their punishment was going to be a slow and painful one. He couldn't remember how he got to the well, the well that they had placed him in, or rather hung him in. His body ached and throbbed from his injuries. He'd have hated to see how bad his legs looked under his jeans because he was sure he would have bruises and God only knew what the back of his head looked like. He couldn't feel any blood nor could he see any on his shirt collar so it would appear that the hit to his head hadn't broken any skin but had just knocked him out. However, he couldn't be sure. He had learned a bit of first aid while he had been in the army so he knew he had a concussion, passing out now and again with occasional dizziness when he was awake.

He was chained up, hanging halfway down into the well but still too far from the top so he couldn't reach even if he managed to get free which he soon learned was almost impossible. He had wasted so much time and energy trying to break free the first day and failed every single time he tried. They had chained his hands and feet together while they had strategically hung him, so he was literally trapped. A slow death was definitely their way of punishment. He tried a number of times to break free from the chains, but even if he could get free, he had no idea if he'd be able to climb out of the well as the walls looked like there were no holes for him to bury his fingers into for grip.

He couldn't imagine anyone was looking for him nor could he imagine anyone actually missing him. He had left everyone behind back home and the last time he saw Mia he had literally acted as if she didn't exist. While he was trapped, he couldn't stop himself from replaying the expression she had on her face the last time he saw her. He knew he had hurt her and thinking that he may not ever be found, he hated himself for what he had done. The last time he had seen her and the face he would remember was the day he had caused her pain. He knew she hadn't deserved it, but he had only done it to protect her from him, well, protect himself from falling for her. He should've had the courage to talk to her because now he would never be able to change their last interaction with each other. He had no idea where he was, he couldn't even remember the car ride so he was doubtful anyone would be able to find him. He was trapped and waiting to die.

## 18

Mia knew she would stop at nothing until she found the men who had taken Sage. She couldn't imagine what he must be going through. They could be doing all sorts of horrible things to him, she thought and as much as she tried to distract herself from those kinds of thoughts, she couldn't stop herself. They could have him in a basement somewhere, tied up to a chair and torturing him with knives and tools, maybe even pulling out his fingernails and teeth like Mia had seen in torture movie moments. Or maybe they had been slowly drowning him by constantly shoving his head into a bucket of water. Mia had to stop herself from thinking anything else before she really lost it. She had watched too many crazy movies growing up so she shouldn't let her mind run crazy.

She was lucky enough to have been given footage of

the night Sage had been taken. She watched the footage over and over again, constantly wincing every time she watched Sage get hit. The hit to his head seemed to have caused the most damage because when they had hit the backs of his knees he fell to the floor without any hesitation and without any thought of protecting his face. Mia watched as he stayed limp on the ground. They had picked him up and shoved him into the back seat of their car. She couldn't stand the thought of him being in pain, and she had to find him alive or else all hell would break loose.

She called in the help of Adam, the previous ringleader of the Screaming Demons in Daytona who was the guy they had met when they had first arrived in Florida. She still hadn't left the house due to Fiona's orders, so Adam went to the house to meet her. He rang the doorbell, and when she saw his face, she instantly opened the door for him.

"Please, come in," she said as she gestured him inside. "Thank you so much for coming and offering to help. I really appreciate it, and I'm sure Sage will too," she said.

"It's no problem. I really hope we can catch these guys," he said. Mia hoped so too. She pressed play on the remote, and they both sat in silence as they watched the attack happen. After showing him the footage, she was relieved to find out that he could identify the men. She was even more pleased when he also told her he knew where to find them.

"Are you sure you can bring them in?" Mia asked.

"Definitely. I've seen them around recently. They must be extremely confident that they won't be caught," he replied.

"Perfect. I need you and however many men you need to go out there and bring them to the bar. We need to deal with this immediately so we can find Sage. Who knows what they've already done to him." She choked up at the end of her sentence, almost allowing herself to think of the horrible things the Omens were capable of doing.

She had been involved with them and had once been a victim herself. She knew they would kill Sage, especially once she had learned about the incident on the night he had been taken. He should've known better, she thought, he should've known they wouldn't have let him get away with what he had done. She knew that from experience and so did he. Why had he been so stupid, she had asked herself.

"Yes, of course," Adam said. "I'll call the men I need and go now," he said as he got up to leave.

"Thank you, Adam. I would appreciate it if you could bring them in after working hours, of course. I don't want to cause a scene, but if anything were to happen to our guests while we have them, I would hate for there to be any witnesses," she said. Adam nodded, getting her extremely obvious hint. Mia was still waiting for Grier who hadn't arrived yet, and she knew that she would control this mission on her own if she had to. Nothing could stop her from finding Sage as soon as possible even if that meant disobeying orders from her boss.

* * *

A COUPLE OF HOURS LATER, Mia got a call from Adam.

"Adam," she answered, "please tell me that you have good news."

"Definitely. They were extremely easy to find. Like I said, they were too confident," Adam replied with a smirk in his voice. Mia agreed. Clearly, they thought that being part of the Omens meant they would be untouchable, but they were going to find out just how wrong they were. She had been at the house, patiently waiting, not only for Adam's call but still for Grier. She thought of the moment she could confront the men who had taken Sage. She wanted to look them in the eyes as she caused them pain. The anger inside her had constantly been growing since Adam had left and she was just about ready to kill someone. Karma's a bitch, she thought.

Although she had been mad at Sage just a few days before, her body had become consumed with hate toward the Omens. She could hardly remember what she was mad about when it came to Sage. Well, she could, but it all seemed pretty pointless now. His life hung in the balance, and Mia had to forget all her hurt for now and just focus on finding him. That was her main thought - she needed to find Sage before it was too late.

It's showtime, she thought to herself as she placed her switchblade in her back pocket. She had started to carry it around with her after she had been attacked. She had no idea if she'd use it but if anything happened, she knew she could.

She left the house, locking up behind her. It was only a few days ago that she thought Sage had run off with another woman. She thought that he had left her more alone than ever. It was crazy how things changed. She never thought she could be a killer, but now that thought didn't seem so stupid after all.

She made sure she called for a taxi while she was inside, just in case someone was waiting to attack her, so when she saw the taxi pull up outside of her house, she decided to run and get in as quickly as possible.

She arrived at the bar not long after the call from Adam. She wanted to get answers, and she wanted them as soon as possible. She hesitated just outside the closed bar doors. She noticed that almost all the lights had been switched off. It was clear that everyone knew that what was about to happen had to stay between those involved so no attention could be brought to the bar that was out of character.

She appreciated the effort from her men, knowing she had the right group of guys to rely on in her moment of need. She knew they weren't doing it just for her though. They wanted Sage back just as much as she did. They had all grown to love him and his character. He would always greet them and ask them about their personal life. He wanted to build a bond with them that was stronger than business, and he had definitely succeeded. No one else within the Screaming Demons had made the effort he had, and they looked up to him for it.

She proceeded to knock on the closed doors. She had never been given a key as she had never had to be there after hours.

"We're closed!" someone yelled from inside. They knew to expect her, but clearly, they had to keep everything under control and keep everything looking normal.

"It's Mia," she said, and within seconds the doors were unlocked, and she could see for herself what was going on.

She walked into the bar and stopped just near the entrance as the doors were closed and locked behind her. She counted twelve of her men spread out in front of her. They had placed themselves in a semi-circle, there being a space left open as she entered so she could see directly into the middle of the room. The two men had been tied up and placed on two chairs in the center of the room. As she walked closer to them, she could tell that the men were probably around her age. She couldn't help but pity them for they had probably continued down a path that she was fortunate enough to get away from.

She couldn't help but go back to the memory of her attack in the alley. Staring at the men before her, she wanted to not only get revenge for Sage but for herself. She had never been the same after her attack, and she had the Omens to thank for that. They looked at her, completely helpless, placed before her like a prize, a sacrifice. She could lick her lips like a hunter would just before they dug their teeth into their prey. Both men looked twice her size so she wasn't surprised that both of them together could've taken Sage down with weapons, but she knew that in one-on-one hand combat they wouldn't have stood a chance. She could tell that they had been beaten up a bit. One had a cut and bruised lip while the other had a black eye slowly starting to form. She couldn't help but smirk in their direction. Soon those would not be the only injuries they had, she thought.

"Hello, boys," she said to her men. They all looked at

her waiting for a command. They were ready to attack. She couldn't be sure if they had respect for her the way they respected Sage, but today she would gain it because she was definitely a force no one would want to mess with.

"Looks like we have a problem to solve," she said as she stared down at the two men placed before her.

They smirked at her without saying a word. She wanted to smack the smirks off of their faces.

She started to walk closer to them, wanting to place herself right in front of them. She knew she was a small woman, and to them, she probably didn't look very aggressive. Little did they know the amount of rage pulsating throughout her small, tiny body. She was just about ready to pounce on anything that just breathed the wrong way.

"Where is Sage?" she demanded after a few seconds had passed. She decided she would take it slow and then when they least expected it, go batshit crazy on their asses. She knew it was bound to happen. They weren't going to give in to her that easily.

The men continue to stare at her.

"Sage? Who's Sage?" one asked as the other roared into laughter. Soon they were both laughing in her face.

Some of her men had also started edging forward. It was clear that Mia wasn't the only one desperate for the location of Sage, and she knew she had the right people on her side.

"Easy guys," she said as she turned to her men. "We need answers first before we do anything to our guests." She turned back to the two men who hadn't taken their eyes off of her but had stopped laughing. She continued to move closer to them, and just as she was a few feet away from them, they both spat at her.

She was just far enough away for the spit to fall at her feet, but she couldn't help but feel the rage that shot up inside of her. The room went red in her eyes, and she wanted answers. She wanted respect and most of all she wanted the men to pay for what they had done to Sage and to her.

She knew she would have to let a side of herself out that no one had seen before. She had always been looked at as if she were just a little girl, but she would prove that she was a lot more powerful than anyone thought.

She reached into her back pocket to pull out the switchblade she had placed there. At the sight of the knife, she could sense the change in the atmosphere. Everyone knew she wasn't there to mess around anymore. Even her men watched her carefully as she made her next move.

She then slowly walked over the spit and closed in on one of the two men, the one who had started laughing first. She wanted to hurt him the most.

Soon she had the blade crammed into the soft spot just below his jaw. Just one wrong move from her part could send the blade right through his cheek and maybe with a little more pressure right into his eye. It would bring Mia a lot of pleasure if she caused both of the men some pain, but not yet, she reminded herself.

"Test me you swine! Now tell me, where have you hidden Sage?" She kept her voice strong and harsh, letting spit escape her mouth so it could land on his face, making sure they knew she wanted answers and was no longer accepting their behavior. The man winced as the knife started to cut into the first few layers of his skin. She watched as fear flashed before his eyes. She had gotten the response she was definitely looking for.

"We've placed him in a well just passed Omen territory. The area is surrounded by Omens. There is no way you'd be able to get to him without being caught," he replied as carefully as he could, possibly trying to keep the blade from cutting any further into his jaw. Mia could see blood slowly starting to trickle down his neck. A small cut would have to do for now. She removed the blade. As much as she would have loved to injure both men, she had the information she wanted, and she had to get out of there and head straight for Sage. She had no idea what kind of state he could be in, and she could not risk waiting any longer to rescue him.

"Let's fall out!" she yelled.

Mia and her men headed out of the bar, leaving the Omens men tied up where they were. They would deal with them later. Adam, who had stayed to fight alongside everyone else, announced that he knew where the well that they were referring to was and he could lead them all there. It didn't take long for them all to hop onto a bike and head out. Mia also found a bike to use and so she hopped on. Sage didn't know she knew how to ride and neither did the other men. They watched in shock as she started the bike, roaring it to life, and sped off behind Adam. The rest of the men soon all fell behind her. She would not miss out on finding Sage and bringing him home. And she could no longer wait for Grier's arrival.

## 19

The bike ride felt good to Mia. She managed to clear her mind a little. She had gotten a little foggy with the adrenaline rushing through her veins. She was filled with excitement and anxiety. She was excited to now know exactly where Sage was but she was definitely anxious about what state she would find him in. Had one of her ideas been right? She hoped not as they were on the extreme side of torture and she prayed Sage hadn't gone through anything like that. She knew he would be further traumatized because even though he wouldn't admit it, she knew he still relived the trauma from Afghanistan. She could some- times hear him moaning and screaming from his room while he slept. She hadn't dared say anything nor had she ever tried to wake him but it explained why he always had to have a shower in the morning. She had looked in on him once and he was covered in sweat. She knew that this trauma would just add to it. It was impossible for it not to and he'd be lying if he told anyone he was fine after all of it. Anyone who had been attacked and trapped somewhere under torture would be traumatized. She knew she was still traumatized by her attack, and that hadn't lasted long when he had shown up.

Once they arrived, they couldn't possibly keep their presence a secret due to the mass amount of bikes. The noise of their bikes made their presence known before they had even arrived. The Omens had time to plan a line of defense.

Mia knew anything could happen and they were prepared for anything, so when the first few unexpected shots went off, everyone immediately took cover so they could reach for their own guns. She, however, didn't have a gun and had to stay covered under the bike she had used while her men all spread out.

She could make out only six guns as she watched the Omens firing off their guns in the distance. Their six were no match for her twelve, and they knew it when they started to slowly back away. It didn't take long before her team had cleared the area and all the Omens had either been caught or were hiding. Her team spread out and slowly made sure that all the Omens were caught and accounted for. She didn't have time to get answers from them as time was running out so she decided she would lead in the hunt for Sage.

The area was dark as nightfall had already started to settle for the night. She could not see her hand when she raised it in front of her face so she knew she'd have to look carefully when she got the all-clear.

As soon as the area was secure, she started to call out for Sage.

"Sage?" she called. Her flashlight scanning the ground as she continued to take the lead. She scanned the ground around her as she slowly led them into the field where Sage was hidden.

Her men were all searching the property for the well alongside her. As she continued to call out for him, she could make out the movements of everyone around her, she could make out the crunch of dried grass beneath her feet as she walked the field. She could smell mud as she sometimes found herself stepping into wet areas. It was clear that most of the grass had been either dried out or burnt. She could only hope that if there were a fire it hadn't involved Sage. The thought terrified her. All heads were down and flashlights scanning the area, moving and picking up anything that came across their paths, making sure Sage wasn't beneath them.

They continued to move forward in a row equally keeping up with each other making sure nothing was missed in the darkness. Panic started building in Mia's body, no one had come across the well yet, and they had no idea how far out it was or if they were even looking in the right direction.

"Sage! Please, where are you?" she called out again, her voice breaking at the end as concern and worry started to flood her body. She didn't want to picture him dead somewhere. She definitely did not want to find him dead either. It would be the worst thing ever if that were to happen. She could feel a slow fall of tears running down her face.

She could only hope they weren't too late since she hadn't gotten any response from her calls.

"I'm here!"

Finally, on her third call for Sage, she could make out a faint sound. It sounded like Sage, it sounded like his voice.

"Sage!" she yelled, this time with urgency. He was alive! She could jump up and down with joy, but she knew she couldn't until she had him in her arms. His voice was faint, so faint that she couldn't make out the direction it had come from. He had fallen silent.

"Do not stop making a noise, okay? We're coming for you. We need you to lead us to where you are so please continue to make any noise you can," she begged him.

Tears had started forming in her eyes again, a sense of relief had already begun to flood through her body. Sage was alive, and soon she would be able to see him.

She continued to follow the noise that Sage kept on making. It stopped sounding like him shouting and turned into groans. She could tell he was in a lot of pain before she even looked, and she was completely terrified of what she might see.

It wasn't long before all twelve men and Mia were standing just next to the well which had been covered in timber. She could not begin to imagine what it must've been like for Sage to have been almost buried considering the well was built on ground level. It must've been so dark down there all alone she thought to herself. When the timber had been removed, Mia shone her flashlight down into the well and was horrified to see the state Sage was in. It was a lot worse than what she had pictured.

She could make out bruises around his hands and feet, which were bare and covered in chains. She wasn't sure if the bruises were due to the chains themselves or because of his attempts to probably try to break free. She knew Sage well enough to know he wouldn't have just accepted his fate. He would've tried to get out. He looked so pale and extremely skinny under his dirty clothes. She knew she needed to get him warm again because she could see his lips were turning blue. It was also clear that they had been starving him. He looked so small and helpless. She could not believe how cruel people could be. She knew that once they had gotten him safely out of the well she would definitely make the Omens pay and it wouldn't just be a cut to one of them. She would hunt every one of them down and cause them all pain, her heart had never been filled with so much anger before.

"Oh my God," she whispered. The tears that had been forming in her eyes started streaming down her cheeks.

"We're going to get you out, okay?" she called down to him as she rubbed her tears off her face. She did not want anyone to see her so vulnerable.

"Please," Sage groaned. His voice cracked, probably from dehydration, she thought. She was breaking inside at the sight of him.

"Don't worry, we're here, and we're not going anywhere without you," she said. As much as she was trying to keep him calm and reassure him that the situation was under control, she had begun to struggle to keep herself together. She wanted him out of there.

After some careful planning, the men had figured out a way of getting him out. They would have to go in themselves so they could get him out without causing him any further injuries. He looked so fragile and weak, they couldn't risk anything else happening to him. Soon rope which had been left behind from the Omens was found, and two men were securely tied and had slowly started to descend into the well where they then proceeded to carefully cradle Sage from both sides just like a newborn child, both placing their arms under his knees and under his arms.

"Careful with his knees. They must be badly bruised after the hit he received," she called out to them. She had to look away as they brought his body to the surface.

"I'm okay, I'm okay," Sage said, although it was clear he was in a lot of pain.

The rest of the men slowly pulled themselves back up. The two men closest to the well took Sage and carefully placed him on the ground while the two men who were in the well managed to climb out.

Without thinking, Mia wrapped herself around Sage, pulling him into her body. His body felt small in her arms, and his clothes were cold and wet while he smelled of urine and feces. She couldn't let go of him though as she continued to cradle his body. She only wanted to hold on to him tighter.

"Thank God you're alive," she whispered softly, softly enough that Sage hadn't heard.

She could not believe she had him safely in her arms once again. Although this had been different from any other experience she had shared with him, she couldn't have felt more grateful for his life as well as her own. Sage had almost died, she knew as she held his body. She could feel so much of his life had been dragged out of him over the past few days, and she knew he would never be the same, but she was grateful that her determination had pushed her through and she had found him. She couldn't bear to think what might have become of him if she had done nothing, if she had tried to forget him altogether the night after the bar. He might not have been there with a beating heart. As she thanked any higher being that was above her, she couldn't help but be grateful for her life too. She had also almost died a few times, and she had still taken her life for granted since she had still gone down the wrong path for far too long before she had managed to get herself back into a place where she could be happy.

She knew Sage felt the same about his life, even if he didn't want to admit it. He had never told Mia about his past, but she had taken it upon herself to do her own research when he first entered her life. He was a good man despite what he thought of himself, and she just wanted to reassure him of that. Over time she hoped that Sage could trust her and let her in but only time would tell when it came to that. Until then she would remain by his side.

"Mia?" someone asked. She looked up and saw her men had gathered around her.

"Yes?" she asked. She wasn't exactly sure who had called her name.

"Grier is on his way," someone said. She could barely focus on anything other than Sage in her arms.

"Oh, good," she replied. It was good that Grier had

landed safely and would soon be on his way to the scene; however, she knew they needed an ambulance.

"Has someone called for an ambulance?" she asked. She didn't think it would be a good idea to move Sage until help arrived. He definitely needed to be checked out and possibly hospitalized.

"Yes, we've called for an ambulance, and one has been sent out already."

"Great, that's just great," she replied.

More tears started running down her cheeks, but they were tears of joy. Sage was alive and in her arms. She could feel him, she could feel him breathing against her chest. She never wanted to let him go. Sage didn't try to fight her off, he didn't say a word instead he just let her envelop him in her arms. To him, it felt like the right place to be after all this time.

Mia knew deep down in her heart that the reason she hadn't been able to move on from Sage after all this time was because she loved him. She had felt it deep within her for so long, but she had kept denying it to herself, she didn't think it was possible to love him after everything, but somehow she could look past it because in her deepest of hearts she knew that she could spend the rest of her life with Sage if he would let her. She wasn't sure a few days ago when she had started asking herself some serious questions, but she knew the answer all along. Sage had been the man she had pictured when she was growing up. He was strong, and she could definitely see that now, he was humble because even after his act in the bar she knew it must've hurt him too. He was just as emotional as she was even if he tried to deny it. He had tried to remain strong in front of her all the time but looking at him in the most vulnerable state she had ever seen him in, she knew that he was just a man in a lot of emotional pain from all his past wounds. He wasn't a man that didn't deserve love, he was a man who needed love most of all because he had deprived himself of it for so long. Mia wondered if he would ever allow himself to feel love again because after all, he was the only one standing in his way.

Mia could hear the sound of sirens echoing out in the distance, help was on its way, and soon Sage would be on his way to recovery. Mia doubted he would ever truly recover from this. She knew he'd act like it, but she had no doubt in her mind that he would eventually need help with dealing with everything. He had been under so much trauma for one person, she thought.

She knew he would have to work through his past to allow himself the chance to fully move forward with his life. She knew it wouldn't be easy and she would be with him every step of the way, but she hoped he would try because she believed that they could have a beautiful life together.

She knew she loved him the more she thought about

it. If she had learned anything from all of what had happened over the last few days, she knew without a doubt that she loved Sage, despite all of his flaws and faults. The ache in her heart had not ceased since he had been missing and it was only when she had him in her arms that she could admit to herself what she had been trying to deny for so long. She was in love with Sage. She couldn't tell him that though so she just continued to hold him while a blanket was wrapped around them.

She could only show her love even if that meant it wasn't returned. She would not be able to live with herself if she denied him the love she felt even if she couldn't tell him.

He was a man who definitely needed love after everything he had been through, and Mia would take the responsibility of giving it to him.

Soon help arrived, and so did Grier. Sage was sent out to the hospital while Grier and Mia went over a few details.

"I'm glad you took the lead and did what needed to be done to find our guy," Grier said. Mia knew she would've searched every country around the world if that's what it would've taken to find him. She knew that as long as she lived, she would do anything for Sage.

"It wasn't a problem. He needed to be found, and I couldn't sit around. It had to be done so he was returned home safely," she said. It was strange for her to talk to

Grier instead of Fiona. She rarely communicated with him as Fiona was more of her boss.

"It took a lot of strength and power to do what you did," he said. It sounded to Mia as though he was trying to compliment her.

"Well, thank you," she replied. She felt pleased with herself. She hoped that now they trusted her a bit more. Surely she had proven herself now.

"You did a fine job. It's me who should be thanking you. Sage is one of the best men I have, and I honestly don't know what I would've done if he hadn't made it out of this alive." She couldn't agree with him more, the thought of possibly losing Sage had crossed her mind so many times, but every time it seemed to hurt her even more.

"I know how you feel. We're all very lucky to have him in our lives," she replied. Grier nodded in agreement. The day was finally over. Mia and Grier both headed to the hospital to keep an eye on Sage for the night. They had gotten him out of the well, but he may be in a lot more danger after what his body had gone through.

Mia stood at the door of Sage's hospital room. He still looked so small and vulnerable in his bed. She could tell that he had lost a lot of muscle mass due to the starvation he had gone through. He was fortunate though to not have suffered from any broken bones. He was banged up pretty bad, but besides a few bruises and a large lump on his head, he should make a speedy recovery, the doctors had told Mia. She didn't know if she should go into his room or not. After a moment of silent deliberation, she entered his room and watched him as he slept. The doctors wanted to keep him overnight for observation, just in case anything happened. Mia knew she couldn't leave him there since she had just gotten him back and so she placed herself next to him in his hospital bed. She was small enough, and due to the meds they had put him on, he didn't stir as she covered both of them with his blanket.

She wanted to remain next to him so she could hear his breathing. She carefully placed one of her hands on his chest so she could feel his heartbeat beneath her fingers. She could feel that he was warm again and not as cold as he had been when she found him. She fell asleep next to him, feeling at peace with his body finally next to hers after their separation. She knew Sage could wake up at any moment and tell her to leave, but she didn't care. She would leave the bed if he wanted, but she would not leave the hospital. She would not let him out of her sight for too long ever again.

# TWISTED INTENTION
~ A billionaire revenge romance series ~
Twisted Beauty
Twisted Love
Twisted Fate

## Mafia's Obsession
~ A hot mafia romance series ~
Mafia's Dirty Secret
Mafia's Fake Bride
Mafia's Final Play

## Screaming Demons
~ An MC romance series full of suspense ~
Rough Start
Rough Ride
Rough Choice
Rough Patch
Rough Return
Rough Road
Rough Trip
Rough Night
Rough Love

## Standalone Contemporary Romance
Billionaire in Vegas
Billionaire Hunt

Billionaire's Game
Billionaire Retreat
Billionaire On Air
A Chance To Love
Somebody To Love
Not Mine To Love


Check out Summer's entire collection at
**www.summercooper.com/books**

# ABOUT SUMMER COOPER

Thank you so much for reading. Without you, it wouldn't be possible for me to be a full-time author. I hope you enjoy reading my books as much as I do writing them.

Besides (obviously!) reading and writing, I also love cuddling my dogs, shouting at Alexa, being upside down (aka Yoga) and driving my family cray-cray!

Get in touch at
hello@summercooper.com
www.summercooper.com

facebook.com/summercooperauthor
instagram.com/summercooperauthor
goodreads.com/summercooper
bookbub.com/profile/summer-cooper